"We divorce in three months."

Thor shook his head. "Six. Minimum. And we marry in four weeks."

Andrea put the chair between them. "That's too soon!"

"Tough."

"The wedding," she gasped, as he hooked a foot around the chair leg and booted it to one side. "It's to be small and intimate."

"Try large and public and at my church." He kept coming. "Any more conditions I should know about?"

She nodded, speaking fast. "It isn't like this is a real marriage or anything. I won't have…be…" Her eyes widened in alarm as he reached her. "No touching!"

"Trust me. There will be lots of touching. Starting now."

Dear Reader,

Okay. I admit it. I'm a sucker for love and weddings and happily-ever-afters. It's sort of an occupational hazard. I love to laugh my way through a book, while shedding the occasional tear. I'm also partial to strong, dynamic heroes who are still capable of sweet, romantic gestures.

The first time I met my husband, Frank, I was dragging home from a convention in San Francisco, totally exhausted. He saw me struggle by his house, high heels over one shoulder, shopping bag-size purse over the other, and hauling my six-ton suitcase behind. He, bless his heart, came charging out on his white steed and carried me the rest of the way home. (Actually, he grabbed a handcart from his garage and loaded me, my suitcase, purse and heels onto it and pulled me the rest of the way home.)

I fell in love with Thor, my hero in *A Wholesale Arrangement*, while writing his brother Rainer's story, *In the Market* (Harlequin Romance #3183, March 1992). I quickly discovered that Thor's my favorite type of man—a heroic, take-charge sort, who's also a pushover for a damsel in distress. He's the kind of man who comes along once in a lifetime. The kind you grab on to with both hands and never let go. Now that I think about it...he's a lot like Frank.

Sincerely,

Day Leclaire

A WHOLESALE
ARRANGEMENT
Day Leclaire

Harlequin Books

TORONTO • NEW YORK • LONDON
AMSTERDAM • PARIS • SYDNEY • HAMBURG
STOCKHOLM • ATHENS • TOKYO • MILAN
MADRID • WARSAW • BUDAPEST • AUCKLAND

Special thanks to:
Bjarne and Judy Anthonsen;
Liv Dahl and Roy Everson,
Sons of Norway Viking Magazine;
Esther Dyer and Karin Larsen;
and Ron Rosella, Rosella's Fruit and Produce.
Your help was invaluable!

ISBN 0-373-03238-2

Harlequin Romance first edition December 1992

A WHOLESALE ARRANGEMENT

Copyright © 1992 by Day Totton Smith.

CHAPTER ONE

"SHE'S WHAT?"

Thor Thorsen kicked aside his chair and surged to his feet, his impressive size instantly dwarfing everything—and everyone—in the room. He slammed his palms onto the desk in front of him and leaned across it. His voice dropped to an ominous rumble. "She's *what?*" he repeated.

"You heard me," Rainer responded, not the least bit intimidated by his older brother's wrath. He lifted a scruffy sneakered foot and rested it on the edge of the gleaming mahogany desk. "Andrea's price-gouging. You know the term 'price-gouging,' don't you? That's when one party has another party at a financial disadvantage and puts the screws—"

"I know what it means." Thor returned fire. "Give me proof. Evidence. You know the term 'evidence,' don't you? That's when one party can substantiate their accusations against another party with documentation." He switched his furious gaze to Rainer's companion. "What do you have, Red? Fair warning. It had better be good."

The fifty-year-old man lifted a nervous hand to hair gone iron gray. "Calling it price-gouging might be a tad strong. I think, maybe."

Rainer snorted and tilted his chair to a precarious two-legged angle. "Yeah, right. Andrea Constantine is as innocent as a lamb and I wear eggplants for slippers." A back-handed swipe knocked his foot off the desk and he scrambled to keep from falling.

"Let him speak or you'll be eating those eggplants, as well as wearing them," Thor informed his brother, ignoring his acrobatic efforts to remain upright. "Go on, Red."

The older man cleared his throat. "That term, er, price-gouging, does suggest a certain deliberation on Miss Constantine's part. And, well, we don't know for certain it is. Deliberate, I mean. I think maybe it could all be a little misunderstanding."

"A little misunderstanding," Thor repeated softly. "Rainer says Andrea's billing our stores twice what her father, Nick, charged us six months ago. *That's* a little misunderstanding?"

Red gulped. "I think maybe...yes?"

"I think maybe no!" Thor glared at his brother. "Evidence I said. Where's the evidence?"

"You want it? I've got it." Rainer's demeanor changed abruptly. He tossed a bulky folder marked "Constantine's Wholesale Produce Market" onto Thor's desk. "Here's a little evidence for you. These are the produce invoices from a year ago, six months before Nick Constantine's death."

Thor sat down and picked up the folder, extracting the pertinent files. They brought back bittersweet memories—memories he'd prefer to forget. Memories he couldn't forget. With bleak determination, he focused on the papers, swiftly absorbing the necessary information. "This would be the month after our contract with Constantine's first took effect."

"Right. And this next piece of evidence—" Rainer sent another folder spinning onto the desk "—is seven months ago, immediately before Nick's death. You'll note some minor fluctuation in prices. But overall, it's within acceptable parameters."

"Lettuce and cucumbers up. That was mid-December. The freeze in central California and the heavy rains in Mexico would account for the increases there."

Rainer's gaze hardened. He heaved the final folder onto his brother's desk. "This is last month's invoices. My last bit of evidence and proof positive."

Thor could guess what was coming, but he glanced through the invoices, anyway. They confirmed his worst fears. "Damn." He rocked back in his chair and closed his eyes. *Why, Andrea? Why couldn't you leave well enough alone? You had to hit out at me, didn't you?*

The increases were huge. He knew simple inflation couldn't come close to accounting for them. No, the reason had nothing to do with business. Anger began to build in him, a hot penetrating wrath that seeped into his veins and spread like quicksilver. His mouth firmed into a taut line as he fought to control it. Andrea always did manage to rouse a strong reaction one way or the other.

"There's more."

"I don't doubt it." Thor rested an elbow on his desk and rubbed a finger across his jaw. "Finish it."

Rainer handed him a graph. "I've charted some of our standard purchases over the past twelve months and compared them to last year's. Just a few of the basics—lettuce, potatoes, things our retail produce markets and Milano's Restaurants get from us on a daily basis."

Thor studied the sharp upward slash of the red line on the graph. "Prices began to skyrocket right after Nick died and are headed straight through the roof." He tossed the chart onto the desk and glanced from Red to his brother. "We can't let this continue. We have to act. Suggestions?"

Red spoke first. "She's a woman, you know."

Both Thor and Rainer stared at the older man.

"She's...she's a woman, you know," he repeated with dogged determination. "I think maybe that could mean something."

Thor fixed his attention on the nervous man. "Such as?" he asked with barely concealed impatience.

"A woman in this business..." Red's brow puckered. "Don't know. Don't seem right somehow. Think maybe we could check to be sure there's been no mistake?"

Thor considered the possibilities for a minute. Andrea deserved the benefit of the doubt. But facts were facts. What legitimate excuse could there possibly be? On the other hand...

"He's right," Rainer reluctantly conceded. "We should be certain before we act."

"Agreed." Thor thought for a moment, then spoke. "Have my secretary call Constantine's main competitor, Produce, Inc. Don't mention Thorsen's. She's a woman calling out of the blue. Have her get the price on a box of bananas, a flat of strawberries and a carton of lettuce."

Rainer lifted an eyebrow. "Clever. If Produce, Inc., gives a better deal to a complete stranger than Constantine's gives to their best customer, we'll know for sure Andrea's price-gouging."

"Red," Thor prompted. "Take care of it right away."

The older man's expression turned gloomy. "Yes, sir. Won't take no time at all."

"Thanks." Thor waited until he was alone with his brother before continuing. "So, tell me the rest. The part you weren't saying in front of Red."

"Never could put one over on you." Rainer leaned forward, his voice grim. "I've heard rumblings from other retailers. It isn't Andrea's prices alone. The quality of the produce is down, too."

Thor's eyes narrowed. "That would explain the phone calls I've received of late. Three different wholesale houses, in addition to Produce, Inc., are after our business. And they're willing to give some major concessions to get it."

"Tough luck we can't take advantage of their offers. At least, not while our contract with Constantine's forces us to buy exclusively from them." Rainer's brows drew together. "If we go anywhere else, we lose the right to service their Milano account."

"We entered into that contract because we could make major bucks supplying produce to Milano's restaurant chain." Thor thumbed through the files on his desk, then decisively flipped them closed. "Unfortunately our contract is with Constantine's, not with the Milanos. In order to keep that account, we *have* to deal with Andrea."

"Can't we sidestep her and cut a separate deal with Milano's?"

Thor shook his head. "I tried that over a year ago and again after Nick's death. Caesar made it clear that his contract's with Constantine's and he isn't interested in any other arrangement."

Rainer didn't hide his annoyance. "Despite the fact we provide him with faster, round the clock service?"

"He's been friends with the family for too long to tolerate change."

Rainer grimaced. "Which takes us back to first base. We buy only from Constantine's, and their good friend Milano buys only from us." He paused. "Still, everybody does make a profit."

Thor tapped the documentation. "You'll notice the last few months our profit's headed straight for Antarctica."

"I agree we can't keep paying top dollar for second-rate produce—"

"Damn right!" Thor cut in. "If something doesn't change, and soon, we'll be lucky to keep the reputations of our retail markets intact, let alone satisfy the Milano's Restaurants account. Tell me where the profit is in that."

A knock at the door interrupted them, and Red stepped into the room. His expression told its own story. "I think maybe price-gouging is the right word, after all," he muttered. With a sorrowful sigh, he turned and left.

Thor's piercing gaze rested on Rainer. "You were supposed to keep an eye on this situation. Why wait so long to tell me?"

"I needed hard facts before I brought it to your attention. Evidence, remember?"

"Evidence?" Thor questioned. "Or the fact that Andrea is your wife's best friend?"

"Leave Jordan out of this—she isn't involved!" Rainer snapped. Then he shrugged. "Your relationship with Andrea is. I don't like having to carry tales about your fiancée."

"Former fiancée," Thor corrected roughly. "And that's no excuse for keeping this information from me."

Rainer smiled skeptically. "You don't think so? Perhaps not. I don't know. But I also waited for the same reason you would have—to give Andrea a chance. What with Nick's death and the amount of work involved in taking sole control of Constantine's, she needed time to get a handle on the business."

Thor swept the papers littering his desk to one side. "She didn't get a handle on *business*. She got a handle on a knife and shoved it in our backs."

"What now?" Rainer asked.

Thor rose to his feet and strode to the window. He leaned against the casing and stared down at the busy Seattle traffic. Why hesitate? He knew what choices were available.

And they were damned few. "Either we pull out of the contract, or I . . . discuss the matter with Andrea."

"What's to discuss?"

Thor ignored his brother's impatience. "Plenty. Like why she's playing games with us, for one."

"Right." Rainer paused. "By the way. Why *is* she playing games with us?"

"I can think of two reasons. It's personal. Or it's personal." He frowned. "I want to be fair. There is one other possibility."

"What's that?"

"The woman could be totally incompetent at running a wholesale produce business."

"So what are you going to do?"

Thor turned and faced him. "I think I'll go have a little chat with Andrea."

BILLS, BILLS, BILLS and more bills. Andrea Constantine studied the listing stack of invoices piled on her desk and fought off an overwhelming sense of panic. Panicking wouldn't do her any good. It might make her feel ten times better, but it wouldn't help. Money would help. Lots of money would help even more. And several truckloads of some large-denominational green stuff would benefit her most of all.

The telephone at her elbow shrilled, and the trucks in her daydream pulled away from the loading dock without having deposited so much as a single penny. She glared at the phone. Thirty more seconds and she'd have been stinking rich. Life, she decided in disgust, had a warped sense of humor. She snatched up the receiver.

"Constantine's," she announced with professional briskness. "Andrea Constantine here."

"Where's my money?" the caller snarled, not wasting time on pleasantries.

There was that annoying, distasteful, *repetitive* "money" word again, being used by an equally annoying, distasteful, repetitive nuisance. "Mr. Hartsworth, I presume," she said, her lips turning down at the corners.

"Damn right! Now where's my money? And no more excuses. I shipped you a truckload of corn and I expect to be paid for it!"

"You shipped me a truckload of worm-ridden mush," she contradicted in a firm voice. "You neglected to ice the corn down properly, and your driver took two full days to get it here."

"How can that be? Yakima's only 140 miles from you!"

"Which makes the trucker's arrival in Seattle forty-eight hours after departing your farm an incredible feat. How'd he go, by way of Hawaii? The heat coming off the tail end of his trailer was unbelievable. It's a wonder we didn't have popcorn!"

"You watch your mouth, little girl."

Little girl? Andrea couldn't help smiling, despite the gravity of the situation. She and Mr. Hartsworth had never met face-to-face or he'd have chosen a different description. At five foot eight, she couldn't be called anyone's "little girl." Oh, well, reasoning with the man might be a futile exercise, but she was determined to give it a try.

"Mr. Hartsworth, the federal inspectors looked at your corn and they agree with me. It's worthless."

"Buffalo chips! Now you listen here. I was supplying your pop with cobs since before you were born. You're lucky I'm willing to work with you at all. So don't try and tell me my business. This isn't some girlie tea party, you know."

"I quite agree—"

He bulldozed on. "If you don't pay up, you'll regret it, inspection or no inspection. I'll see to it that your name is blacker than tar at midnight in a coal mine."

She sat up straighter. That sounded fairly black, all right. And having her name so abused wouldn't help her financial situation any. Still...

The man had dumped bad produce on her, and no one did that. If her father were still living Hartsworth wouldn't have tried such a stunt. The knowledge brought a sharp pang of loss; the knowledge also brought home the painful truth. If her father had taught her the rules of this particular game, she wouldn't be in her present predicament.

Her hand clenched into a fist. One thing she did know with absolute certainty. If she allowed even one supplier to take advantage of her, they'd all start stacking up at her dock ten deep to follow suit.

"I refuse to pay for rotten produce," she announced in no uncertain terms. "And you're not the only one capable of a little tar-tossing and name-blackening."

"Don't give me your lip! You'll pay all right. Because if I put out the word you don't honor your debts, no farmer or broker will ever ship to you again. They'll offload you clear into tomorrow. And I've half a mind to see that they do, maybe more than half a mind."

"You don't have more than half a mind!" she let loose before common sense—or any sense—could prevail. "And don't threaten me. I don't operate well under threats."

"Maybe you'll operate better under promises. Because I promise you, either have a certified check on my desk by five tonight or my lawyer's gonna pick your bank account cleaner than a melon patch after a gleaners' convention! You got that?"

"But—" She winced as his receiver crashed down, ending any further discussion. "That gleaners' convention went through my bank account last week," she murmured disconsolately. "And believe me, they didn't leave a dime, let alone a melon."

She stared at the phone. Maybe, just maybe, she shouldn't have lost her temper. And maybe she shouldn't have antagonized the man. And she definitely shouldn't have allowed her old nemesis, pride, to do all her talking. She rested her chin in her hand. One of these days she'd remember that.

Andrea considered her options. Things were fast going from bad to real bad. If Mr. Hartsworth succeeded in his threats and blacklisted her wholesale market with the other farmers and brokers, she'd go bankrupt. Not that that wasn't a distinct possibility, anyway.

Get with it! she ordered silently. *This isn't how you're supposed to react to problems. Where's your gumption? Where's your drive and ambition? Where's your get-up-and-go?* She groaned. It couldn't have got up and went. It couldn't have. Not now. Not when she needed every ounce of skill, determination and finesse-ful finagling she possessed.

She ran a finger over the prisms hanging from her desk lamp, watching their glittering reflection dance on the walls of her office. All her life she'd looked for the bright side to even the gloomiest of disasters. She'd taken special pride in knowing that somehow, somewhere, she'd find one positive in amongst all the negatives. Until now.

The only positive she could find at the moment was the absolute, positive fact that she'd landed herself in deep, deep trouble. And matters were fast worsening, leaving her helpless to prevent the threatened demise of her company.

She sighed, admitting the sad truth. If Constantine's Wholesale Produce Market was a dike, she wouldn't have enough fingers, toes and elbows to plug all the leaks. She better do something quick, or her father's business would go under.

"If only..." She broke off and shook her head. If only her father hadn't died. If only he hadn't borrowed so much money from the bank. If only she wasn't a woman in a man's world. But Nick did die, he had borrowed money, and she—definitely—wasn't a man. Which left her with one choice and one choice only, to swim fast or drown.

Too bad she only knew the dog paddle.

She let out a small sound of disgust. Honestly. That sort of attitude wouldn't get her beans in this business. Keeping the company viable was important to her. She had something to prove. She wanted to prove to her father that she could succeed in a man's world, despite his feelings to the contrary, and despite the fact he'd never witness her success. And she wanted to prove to herself that she could do it, that she could keep Constantine's, Nick's baby, afloat.

She faced the stack of bills, determination taking hold. "I won't let you down, Dad," she vowed in a resolute voice. "Somehow I'll figure a way out." Taking a deep breath, she reached for the first invoice.

"Andrea? *Cara?*"

She glanced up, the bill fluttering onto the stack, and smiled warmly. Joe Milano. Just what she needed—a long, cool drink of tall, dark and handsome, with a sexy Italian accent to top it off. "Joe! How nice to see you. Come in and sit down."

"I like to see you, too. You look good. Very good." He stepped into the room and gazed around with a touch of bewilderment. "But, ah, where do I sit? You do redecorating, yes? It is... different. Very nice."

With a start she realized that the innumerable files, invoices and reams of paper that had taken up permanent residence in her life also covered every available surface in her office. A hint of color warmed her cheeks. Leave it to Joe to call her particular brand of mass confusion 'redecorating.' Inbred gallantry came as naturally to him as breathing.

"Maybe here," she suggested, striving to lift a stack of order forms from one of the chairs.

"No, no!" Joe exclaimed, easing the burden from her arms with a disapproving frown. "I move them, no problem." He staggered beneath the load, glancing around for a vacant spot to place it. His handsome face mirrored his growing alarm. "Er, *cara,*" he began. "You like these someplace special, yes? You tell me where, please."

She hid a smile. "How about that corner over there?" she suggested, pointing to the least cluttered spot.

"Ah, fine," he murmured in relief. He crossed the room in a few swift strides and dumped the pile onto the floor. Briskly he slapped the dust from his hands and beamed at her. "I am good help. Maybe I move another something, okay?"

She stared at the mess on the floor in secret amusement and shook her head. "You've done more than enough. Thanks."

With a grin, he swept her into a bear hug, thick dark curls tumbling across his brow. "So how you been, huh?" He gave her a lingering kiss on each cheek, his mustache tickling her face. "I miss you. You miss me?"

She laughed, returning his hug. "Always. And I'm not redecorating. This is the stuff from Dad's office, on top of my own. I'm still sorting through it..." Her throat closed over and she broke off helplessly.

Joe slid his hands to her shoulders and studied her, his dark eyes gleaming with instant sympathy. "Poor Andrea. And here I bother you with more troubles. Maybe I come tomorrow, yes?"

"No, no. You're always welcome. Sit down." Besides, she already knew what Joe'd come to discuss—the poor quality of Constantine's produce. More troubles, indeed. She struggled to recover her equilibrium and forced out a smile. "How's Caesar?" she asked, preferring to put off the inevitable.

He relaxed into the chair, running a finger down the sharp crease of his trousers. "My poppa is fine, thank you so much. He ask for you all the time. You not visit for many weeks."

Guilt swept through her. Caesar Milano's arrival in the U.S. twenty-two years ago had coincided with her mother's death, and he and her father had struck up an immediate friendship. Since then, she'd practically lived at the Milano house, the adored honorary daughter of a household overrun by males. A household that, until recently, hadn't included Joe. As the eldest son he'd remained in Italy to care for his aging grandparents, not joining his father until a few years ago. To her delight, Joe had accepted her just as readily as all the other Milanos had, becoming like another big brother.

"I'm sorry I haven't come by. Business. You know how it goes," she offered.

His gaze held reproof. "This is not good, Andrea. Your business, it is too much. I worry about you. Poppa, he worries about you. My brothers, well—" he gestured in dismissal "—they not worry, but they are too stupid to know better."

"I'm sorry," she said sincerely, hastening to add, "Not about your brothers. I mean about not visiting more often."

He studied her for a minute, his brow furrowed in concern. "Er, *cara*. I wonder if maybe you not come because of our little problem?"

"No! Of course it isn't," she denied, the lie bringing a stinging warmth to her cheeks.

He shot her an apologetic glance. "It is embarrassing. I understand," he was quick to soothe. "Your poppa make contract with my poppa. This is fine. Okay. We know Nicky, he do the right thing by us." Joe gave an expressive wave of his hand. "Now Nicky is dead. Poppa, his heart is broken up. He not like to talk business with his little Andrea. You understand?"

All too well. It was the story of her life. Men dealt with that aspect of life and the women kept well away. This conversation wouldn't be happening if she had a brother or a husband. Most of her business problems were a result of that very fact.

"I'm sorry the produce went bad so fast," she said, deciding to cut to the chase. She eyed Joe hesitantly, wondering if he'd mentioned such an awkward, troublesome, wrath-inducing problem to Thor Thorsen. With any luck he hadn't. And with a bit more luck he wouldn't. She cleared her throat. "You, ah, don't need to bother Thor about this. I'll refund you for the produce myself."

Joe drew himself up in apparent insult. "You think I come here with the hand out? No! I come to see how you do. I should not like to say it, *cara*, but you don't look so hot. All this work, it is gonna kill you."

"What do you suggest I do? Joe, I'm a woman."

He grinned, his gaze roaming over her in admiration. "Well, yes. I have noticed this."

She threw him a fierce frown. "That's not what I meant! I mean the prevailing *male* attitude that a woman shouldn't be in the produce business. It's ridiculous. I'm twenty-seven, for Pete's sake. I know what I'm doing." Well, she admitted with painful honesty, she sort of knew what she was doing. "Stop treating me like I have cotton candy between my ears and let's get down to brass tacks."

He stared at her in confusion. "Cotton candy and tacks? What you want with these?"

She smiled. "Business, Joe. Let's get down to business. We need to reach an understanding about our contract."

A long silent moment stretched between them. Andrea could see that he was in a quandary as to how to proceed. To go against a lifetime of conditioning must be difficult, she acknowledged. He might be only in his early thirties, but generations of Milanos had been taught that certain topics were the province of men alone. Clearly this was one of them.

"It is very hard. You understand?" he said at last.

"Yes, I do understand. My father felt the same way. He didn't like women in business, either." She spoke firmly, willing her voice not to falter. "But he's gone now and I'm all that's left. Talk to me, Joe."

He shrugged fatalistically. "Okay. We talk." His dark eyes were very serious, almost bleak, the usual humor and mischief missing. "This contract your father signed, it is good for everybody. We get food fast, we pay only a little more, and we order any time, and Thor, he deliver. This you not do for us. So we are happy. Who give us the produce is not important, so long as it is good produce."

Andrea stared at him in concern. "And it hasn't been. I realize that. I . . . I'm having trouble with my suppliers."

"This trouble, it is over soon?"

"I don't know," she whispered. "I'm doing my best." She swallowed, struggling to push the truth past her pride. "But I guess my best isn't all that good."

His gaze slid away from hers. *"Cara,"* he murmured, "we have problem. The bad produce, it hurt the restaurants. People expect only the very best at Milano's. They start to complain. We hold out many months, but soon, Milano's go *pfft*.'' He gestured downward with his thumbs. ''Down the tub.''

''Tube.''

''That, too.'' He stared at her glumly. ''Our goose, it is cooked?''

''I didn't know,'' she murmured in distress. ''Let me think.''

On every front she faced a brick wall—uncooperative suppliers, poor quality, fierce competition, bad prices, angry buyers and, worst of all, that huge loan with those staggering payments. For her father's sake, for all he'd sacrificed for Constantine's, she'd desperately try to save the business. But without a door in those brick walls, she didn't know how to do it.

The answer came to her. She hated it as an alternative, but she was fast running out of options. If she couldn't save Constantine's, she could at least help the Milanos. A man could succeed where she failed. A man familiar with the business would have a chance of turning things around.

That man was Jack Maxwell. He ran a small wholesale produce business that specialized in restaurant accounts. And he was interested in expanding. He called her on a regular basis offering to buy Constantine's. At a ridiculously low price, true, but it *was* a solution. There'd only been one hitch to his proposition.

She glanced at Joe, requiring more facts before she proceeded. ''Our contract hasn't changed, has it? It's still between the Milanos and Constantine's, right?''

''Correct,'' he agreed.

''If...if Constantine's was sold, the deal would continue with the new owner, not with the Thorsens?''

Joe looked bewildered. "Yes. We have contract with you. You have contract with Thorsen. This mean we stay with you, er, the new owner. Why you ask?"

So Maxwell's one condition—that Constantine's would retain the Milano account—could be met. It also meant that the Thorsens would be left out of the deal because Jack wanted to supply the Milanos directly. *Thor, forgive me,* she thought unhappily before speaking. "It's simple, Joe. If there's no other way—" and she'd begun to believe there wasn't "—I'll sell Constantine's."

Silence reigned.

Then Joe leapt to his feet, launching into speech. "No! This is no good. It is family business. How you sell family business? No, no. I not ask such a thing. Poppa, he not ask such a thing. My brothers—" he snorted "—they probably ask, but I smack them upside the head for being stupid."

Andrea couldn't help it. She laughed. For a minute Joe stared at her, uncertain whether or not to take insult at her amusement. A frown creased his brow. Then his lips twitched and he grinned.

"You think that is funny, huh? I defend your honor to my brothers and you laugh at me?" He crossed to her desk and edged his hip onto one corner. The huge pile of bills wobbled precariously before toppling to the side. Invoices spewed in a white-and-pink flood across the desk and onto the floor.

"The way things are right now, it's either that or cry. And I'm fresh out of tears." She reached for his hand. "It isn't because of Milano's alone that I might sell. There are other factors. Factors I can't control." Like her supply problems and that loan from the bank.

"You maybe discuss these factors?"

"No, I maybe don't discuss these factors."

He leaned closer. "What you say to a little bribe? Some of my cannoli, perhaps?"

"That's not fair!" She gave him a wounded look. "You know how much I love cannoli."

"Of course you love my pastry. This is because Italians make good chefs. *I*," he pronounced without modesty, choosing to interpret her words in his own inimitable fashion, "make great chef." His admiring gaze drifted to her hair and he reached out to snag a soft curl. "This is very good. You love pastry. Me, I love blondes."

"And brunettes and redheads," Andrea added dryly, long used to his flattery.

"Well, yes," he admitted with a broad grin, not a bit abashed. "But blondes!" He covered his heart with his hand and sighed. "These are my favorites."

"Every last one of them," she agreed.

"Ah, *cara*," he reproached. "Finding the good woman is *much* hard work. You marry me and I don't look no more! What you say, huh? We marry and fix all this trouble with your business somehow. No problem. I make you very happy."

To her amazement, she was tempted to accept. Which gave her a clue to how desperate she was. She adored Joe, but not in that way. Gently she set about dissuading him. "I don't think so," she said, then lied without compunction, "You see, I don't like children."

For a minute he simply sat and stared at her. "What you mean you don't like children?"

She shrugged. "Just that. I don't like them."

"Not one?" he demanded, horrified. "Not even little ones? How can this be? You pull on my leg, yes?"

"No, I haven't touched your leg." She smiled in mock innocence. "You see why it won't work."

He closed his eyes, a martyred expression on his face. "Okay, fine, *cara*. I make very big sacrifice. For other woman, no way. But for you, I wait three whole months. You learn to like just the little boys and I marry you. What you say?"

What could she say? Andrea ground her teeth, laboring to find the words to vent her outrage. Then she saw his mustache quiver slightly, a rakish gleam dance in his dark eyes, and knew she'd been had. They both burst out laughing.

He yanked her from the chair and into his arms. "Your face!" he exclaimed. "It is very funny, your face."

"You're lucky you have a face left," she retorted. " 'You learn to like just the little boys.' Get real."

"You should not tell a lie. You do it very bad," Joe reprimanded.

She wrinkled her nose. "Why don't you teach me how to do it good?"

"I teach you anything you like." He lifted a brow. "What you say, huh? We start first lesson right now. I teach you how to—"

"I realize it's a cliché, but it does seem fitting," a deep authoritative voice cut in. "Am I interrupting something?"

CHAPTER TWO

"THOR!" ANDREA GASPED. She struggled to pull free of Joe's embrace, something that proved unexpectedly difficult to accomplish. "I—you—we—"

"Why, Thor Thorsen. Nice to see you again," Joe said, and grinned, his arm locking around Andrea's waist. "You like something?"

"Yes. I'd like something." In two strides he crossed the room. In two seconds he parted Andrea from Joe. And within two heartbeats he ushered a vehemently protesting Joe from the office. Then he turned and faced Andrea.

She stood before him, aware of feelings she thought long dead coming slowly, painfully, to life. It had been one full year since she'd last seen this man, her former fiancé. Three hundred and seventy-five days, to be precise. He looked exactly the same—still the Norwegian thunder god and still thunderous.

How could she have forgotten so many of the little details about his appearance? she wondered, staring freely. Or *had* she forgotten? Perhaps she'd buried the memories, afraid to confront all she'd spurned.

His hair was a rich gold, the stubborn waves burnished with a hint of auburn. He measured several inches over six feet, his shoulders and chest straining against his business suit. When he stood as he did now, his feet firmly planted and his arms folded across his chest, everything about him spoke of power and control. Especially of control.

She met his intense blue eyes with trepidation, her gaze sweeping over his sharply angled face. His broad intelligent brow gave way to high cheekbones and a strong determined chin, his wide mouth set in taut lines. But the most fascinating and incongruous feature of all was the small gold hammer earring he wore in his left ear. The mark of Thor. A mark she'd always associated with crushing strength and power.

All in all, a dangerous animal, she remembered with a touch of apprehension, his fierceness barely held in check by a superficial sophistication.

He stood motionless before Andrea's scrutiny, giving her time to look her fill. And she knew why. The more she saw, the more dismayed she became. Without saying a word, he'd put her squarely on the defensive.

"A suspicious man might read something into your little embrace with Milano," he commented, a slight smile edging his mouth.

Andrea returned his smile. She wouldn't be intimidated by this man. She wouldn't. At least, not much. "And are you a suspicious man?"

"Very." His smile grew, turning almost predatory. "Have I reason to be?"

A heavy pounding from the office door interrupted them. Before Andrea could move, Thor responded, swinging it open. His broad shoulders filled the narrow aperture, barring entrance. "What?" he barked.

"Er, *cara,*" came a muffled voice from the far side of the human wall. "Everything, it is all right? No problem?"

She debated her response for all of five seconds. Why borrow trouble? No point in risking Joe's near-perfect features for a momentary satisfaction. Not when the momentary satisfaction would undoubtedly go to Thor. "No problem, Joe."

Brown eyes bobbed up over Thor's restraining arm. "I see you later, okay? We discuss more our, er, discussion."

"Fine."

"Ciao."

"Yeah, right," Thor muttered, and firmly closed the door.

Andrea frowned. "You have a very strange way of treating your customers. Milano's Restaurants still *is* your customer, isn't it?"

"Last time I checked," he confirmed.

"Aren't you worried he'll be offended and demand we terminate our contract with you?"

"Isn't that the whole idea?"

She hesitated, confused. Thor never said anything without purpose. She might not understand it at the time, but he was the most precise, exacting, exasperatingly direct individual she'd ever met. So, if he suspected Joe might jump to another supplier, and if the only way that could happen was if she sold...

"You think you're about to lose the Milano account?" she guessed, fighting for calm.

"I *know* I'm about to lose the Milano account, and I know who to thank for it."

She stared at him, frozen, as her mind raced to analyze the various possibilities behind his accusation. Because it *was* an accusation. How could he have found out about the possible sale of Constantine's so soon? She frowned. It didn't make sense. She'd only decided to explore that option today. Perhaps Jack Maxwell had been indiscreet, spreading word of his interest in Constantine's and the Milano account. "How did you know I might—"

The pounding resumed at her office door and Thor's eyes gleamed with a dangerous light. "Persistent, isn't he?"

She hid behind mild amusement. "It's silly I know, but most people who knock on that particular door do so in the hopes of speaking to me. I assume you have a logical explanation for why they—he—can't do that?"

"Yes, I do." He opened the door a full six inches. "What?"

"Er, *cara*..." a familiar voice began again.

Andrea struggled to keep her expression perfectly serious. Matters were serious. It was Joe she couldn't take seriously. "Yes?"

"I see you later, when? You forget to tell me this."

"Tomorrow. Here. Nine o'clock."

"Okay, good. I see you tomorrow. Here. Nine o'clock." A concerned face appeared beneath Thor's armpit. "You have more files to move, yes? No problem. I take care of it right away."

This time she did smile. Actually she grinned. "No. Thanks, anyway."

"No?"

"No," Thor said in a tone that could have blistered paint. The face backed hastily away. "Okay, fine. *Addio.*"

"So long, goodbye, it's been great, and see you later. Much later." Thor shut the door just shy of a slam.

He turned around and Andrea busied herself restacking the bills scattered across her desk. If she dared laugh, she'd be in deep trouble. Because if she was any judge, one heck of a storm was brewing across the room. The air practically crackled with electricity. Her thunder god had returned with a vengeance.

"You were saying?" she prompted.

"The Milano account."

She smiled her sweetest smile. "Are you sure Joe shouldn't sit in on this? After all, if it concerns the Milanos..." She gulped at his expression. If she was very, very smart, she'd stay very, very quiet. Let the typhoon run its course and pray she survived the blow.

Visibly restraining his temper, he spoke. "I've received a number of phone calls of late."

Her stack of bills grew taller. "Okay, I'll bite. From whom?"

"Caesar Milano, for one."

Andrea studied him warily. It couldn't be unusual for him to get a phone call from Joe's father. After all, the Thorsens supplied Milanos' Restaurants. She had a feeling she knew what this might be about—and it wasn't the sale of Constantine's.

"And?" she asked.

"It was the first time anyone's ever accused me of cheating them. I didn't like the experience."

A timid knock interrupted them yet again, and Andrea almost screamed in nervous reaction. For an unnerving moment, Thor stared at her through narrowed suspicious eyes, then walked to the door and casually braced a shoulder against the wooden panel.

"Are you sure you didn't misunderstand him?" she protested. "I can't believe Caesar actually thought you were cheating them."

His gaze grew wintry. "He did and he does. My prices, he claims, are exorbitant, my quality shoddy. Since it can't be the fault of his precious Andrea, it must be my doing."

"I'll speak to—"

"I've also received complaints from the managers of our stores." He ignored the louder knock emanating from behind him and continued, "Care to guess why?"

"No." She didn't have to guess. She knew.

"I'll tell you, anyway."

"Er, *cara*," a muffled voice called.

Thor settled his shoulder more firmly against the door. "The produce my markets have received of late is inferior. Their charges are up and their sales are down."

Join the club, she almost said. "Yes, well—"

"You supply us with produce. *All* of our produce. Since we can't buy anywhere else, our quality reflects your quality. And our prices reflect the prices you charge us. It's a tarnished reflection, my sweet. Very tarnished, indeed."

The doorknob rattled. "Andrea, you open up please?"

"Andrea does not please," Thor said in a voice sufficient to blast through three oak doors, let alone one. He stuck a hand in his pocket and pulled out a thick piece of paper. Unfolding it, he tossed a large graph onto her desk. The neat pyramid of bills she'd built collapsed with a soft *poof.* "Explain this, if you can."

She picked up the paper and studied it curiously. "A pricing chart? This looks like..."

Damn. It looked like a graph of her produce charges for the past year. And according to all the spiked red lines, her prices didn't chart too well. This had nothing to do with selling Constantine's, she decided, relaxing a little. Her relief was short-lived.

Thor straightened away from the door and walked toward her, barely suppressed fury in every line of his massive body. "I didn't believe it at first. Not of you. I couldn't credit the possibility that you were guilty of price-gouging."

She dropped the graph and sprang to her feet. "I hear a but in that statement. For your information, I'm *not* guilty of price-gouging!"

"So I compared your prices with another wholesaler," he continued as though she hadn't interrupted. He placed his hands on her desk and leaned forward. "You're so far out of line with the competitors, it's beyond beyond."

She inched away. "There's a reasonable explanation."

"And I saw it here today!" he shot back, knocking the graph and several dozen bills to one side. "You're in cahoots with Milano. You want to deal directly with them again by acing out the middle man." His voice dropped to a low growl. "In case you've forgotten, that middle man's me, sweetheart. And—trust me on this—I don't take that sort of loss well. Not well at all."

Ignoring a stab of fear, she hurried around her desk and planted herself directly in front of him. Her height wasn't sufficient to go eyeball-to-eyeball, but it was close enough. He'd listen. She'd see to that.

"You're wrong!" she informed him in determined tones. "Dead wrong."

"Am I?" He reached out and traced a finger down her cheekbone, drawing a response more unwelcome than unexpected.

She pulled away, furious that she still felt anything for him. He must have read her reaction. His eyes darkened and he lowered his head, his mouth hovering inches from hers. For a fleeting moment she thought he might kiss her. Then his expression closed over and he folded his arms across his chest, fixing her with a stern gaze.

"Prove it," he said.

If only he wasn't so tall and so broad—and so male. If only she could pull her scrambled senses together and approach this argument logically. Thor would listen to reason, if she could *find* her reason.

"It doesn't make sense," she forced herself to say. "The Milanos get much better service from you than from us. You're faster and you're willing to deliver twenty-four hours, seven days a week. They even get better variety because you special-order items we wouldn't normally carry. Besides, we net much more off Thorsen's than we could supplying Milano's Restaurants directly."

He laughed without humor. "I know. I have the receipts to prove it!"

Desperation edged her words. "The Milanos order split cases. Each restaurant requires something different, and it's a dozen of this and six of something else. It means more manpower than it's worth. You order full cases and in huge quantities. And because you have all your retail markets to service, supplying Milano's Restaurants, as well as your stores, works out perfectly. We like it that way. We aren't out to cancel your contract."

Guilt touched her. Unless she sold Constantine's to Jack Maxwell. Thor would lose his contract if that happened. She brushed the thought away. Maybe he wouldn't. She'd find an alternative. Of course she would.

"If you're not trying to break the contract, then what the hell—"

Without warning, the office door flew open, and Joe, followed by her head salesman, Marco, and two of her huskier employees, piled into the room.

"Er, *cara*," Joe began, peering around suspiciously.

"I don't believe this," Thor muttered. "We have business to discuss, Andrea. Uninterrupted business. Now. Do you have a place where that's done? Because we're not accomplishing anything here."

"We'll use Dad's office. Give me two minutes to take care of this and I'll be right with you." Not saying another word, Thor left the room. Andrea fixed her gaze on a sheepish Joe and sighed.

Marco spoke up. "Sorry about this, Ms. Constantine." He gave Joe a disgusted look. "*Somebody* thought you needed help. Though the day you need rescuing from Mr. Thorsen is the day they plant me six feet deep."

"Thanks, Marco." She waited until her salesman and his workers left before addressing Joe, her voice stern. "It's all right. Honest. You can stop playing the overly protective brother. Thor's here to discuss business. That's it. He's not threatening me. He's not frightening me. He's not harming me in any way.''

"He does not make the pass at you?" Joe suggested irrepressibly.

She wished! Andrea closed her eyes. She didn't really mean that, did she? She'd struggled so long to suppress the memories of her time with him. It hurt too much to remember the wonder of it—being in his arms, having his lips teasing hers, knowing the special warmth of his love. He was a man of passion who'd lit an answering passion within her. She dreaded to think that even a tiny spark of that desire remained.

She forced herself to answer Joe's question. "No. That ended a long time ago."

He shrugged. "You should tell this to him. I think he is still in love with you. Perhaps you love him, too?"

"You're wrong," she denied. She couldn't afford to care. Not again.

"Maybe. Maybe, no." At her glare, he held up his hands, dropping the issue. "You sure I should not stay?"

"I'm sure."

"Okay." He crossed to her side and tilted her chin up, studying her expression. "You be careful, *cara*. He is angry. It is not good, him being angry with you."

She offered a reassuring smile. "Thor won't hurt me."

"He did this already," Joe said in a serious voice. "I see you tomorrow. We talk more about our little problem at that time, yes?"

"Yes." She nodded in agreement.

Satisfied, Joe dropped a kiss on the tip of her nose and left the room. Andrea leaned against her desk and fought for strength. Today, it would seem, was her day for problems. She straightened. Now to take care of the biggest of them.

She walked down the hall to where Thor waited. All the offices were located on the second story at the far end of the building. And though each overlooked the cavernous main floor of the warehouse, her father had occupied the corner one. She rarely came in here. The room had always been Nick's private domain, and not even his death could change that.

Thor, she noted sourly, seemed right at home. Huge picture windows enabled him to survey not only the warehouse floor, but the docks, as well. He stood at the window, as her father often had, his legs spread wide, his arms folded across his chest, observing the bustle below.

"I see your *friend* is leaving," he commented, not turning around.

"Can you say that without a sneer?" she asked. "Joe *is* a friend and has been for a lot of years."

"He's in love with you."

"He's concerned about me," she corrected. "And wouldn't like to see me hurt. And I care about him..."

"Care enough to ensure I didn't mess up his face, is that it?"

"Yes." Why deny it? If she'd called to Joe for help, a scuffle would have ensued, with Joe, unquestionably, coming out the worse for wear. "Would you have messed up his face?" she asked, curiosity getting the better of her.

He turned. "I gave it serious consideration."

"Why?"

Humor glinted in his eyes. "I believe it was an inexplicable possessive urge."

"He hugged me."

"And I almost flattened his nose."

"We're not engaged any longer," she pointed out.

"I still want you."

The quietly spoken words hung between them. They shocked Andrea. They shocked her, excited her and frightened her all at the same time. She'd always known Thor was a direct man. She shouldn't be surprised when he chose to prove it. But that didn't change anything. If Thor still wanted her, it was only because she represented a challenge. He was feeling a momentary urge to win what he'd failed to win before.

Time to move on to safer ground. "We have business to discuss," she said. "Perhaps we should discuss it." The lesser of two evils, she acknowledged. But noting the grim expression that wiped every hint of desire from Thor's face, she wondered if flinging herself into his arms might not have been the better solution.

He approached her. "Fine. Business it is. You're overcharging us, Andrea, and it's got to stop. I could go to any of the other wholesale houses and get better produce at much better prices."

She stared up at him in alarm. "You'd lose our Milano account if you did that."

He nodded. "True. But it's fast reaching the point where the Milano account isn't profitable. We've lowered our markup in order to keep them happy. But between what you're charging us and what the Milanos end up returning, we're losing too much money." He tilted his head to one side and studied her. "Why are you doing it? Revenge? You dumped me, remember? I should be the one after blood."

She struggled to keep her composure. "I remember. And for your information, I'm not deliberately overcharging you."

"Pull the other one, sweetheart. I checked. Your prices are so high there isn't any other explanation."

Nick's phone rang and Andrea groaned. This was getting ridiculous. Was she allowed no peace? She grabbed the receiver. "What is it?" she snapped. She closed her eyes and nodded. "Okay, put him through. Mr. Thomas?"

The voice on the other end of the line assaulted her ear, and she held the phone farther away. "But I explained to Mr. Hartsworth." She turned her back to Thor and spoke urgently into the phone. "I refused his corn because it was— No! I won't pay for bad produce, and that's just what he tried to dump on me."

She listened to the lawyer's blistering comments, her own anger rising by the minute. "You can't do that. It's slander! If Mr. Hartsworth causes me to lose so much as one farmer or broker I'll..." At his pithy retort she slammed down the phone.

"Problem?" Thor inquired idly.

"I hate that lawyer!" she announced, glaring at the offending instrument.

"Ah, a lawyer problem."

She froze, aware of how much he must have learned from that one unfortunate conversation. "Not at all," she claimed with more pride than honesty.

A grin eased the corners of his mouth, and observing it, she felt a sharp intense yearning flower to life. He took another step closer and dropped his hands on her shoulders. His touch felt good. It felt right. How could it be so wrong?

"You," he murmured, "are a liar."

"I'm not! I—"

"—can never meet my eyes when you spit out a whopper."

She forced her gaze from the top button of his shirt up to his chin. "Everything's fine," she informed the tiny cleft. She made it to his nose. "Perfect, in fact."

"Higher, brown eyes."

One glimpse of electric blue and she began to babble. "I'm not price-gouging. Honest, I'm not. I'm having a small supply problem." His eyes narrowed. "Okay, okay! I'm having a major supply problem. I'm not my father, and the farmers and brokers who sell to me know it. They're trying to dump their seconds on me. The junk Hartsworth sent couldn't even be called that."

"Did you have the inspectors in?"

"Yes." Resisting the urge to curl up in his arms took every bit of her determination. But resist she did. "They side with me on this. The problem is, if I call them too often, the shippers refuse to deal with me at all. I can't win."

"What about their prices?"

She might as well tell him everything. Confession cleansed the soul, didn't it? Hers could use a good spring cleaning. "Through the roof. A woman in this trade is fair game, I guess."

His eyebrow shot up. "I find it hard to believe your suppliers are trying to put you out of business."

Her mouth curved into a bitter smile. "Oh, they aren't. My *competitors* are trying to put me out of business, and they use every dirty trick they can think of to accomplish it. My *suppliers* are trying to dump their rotting banana peels on me at top prices."

Thor's gaze turned thoughtful. "So costs are up, quality down, and business, I don't doubt, is off."

"Yes."

"Okay, that explains the price-gouging. Now explain Milano's presence. If the two of you aren't cooking up a private deal, why was he here?"

Andrea stared at him in appalled silence, delicate color warming her cheeks. How did she answer that? Simple. She didn't. If she relayed Joe's complaints, Thor would be...upset. And not with the Milanos. She'd be the one receiving the fallout. Nor could she mention the various alternatives she'd discussed with Joe to solve her problems—such as selling Constantine's.

"You look pretty guilty for someone with nothing to hide."

She grappled for an excuse. "He came for a visit. I'm an old friend of the family's, you know."

"And?"

Suddenly she remembered their embrace, the one that had been such a hit with Thor. "And it's personal." She gave her best imitation of a Mona Lisa smile. It felt very strange.

He lifted a single tawny eyebrow. "Your eyelids are at half-mast again," he murmured. "Which means it's not personal. Business?"

Her gaze jerked to his in alarm. "I—you—he—"

"Business," he said with satisfaction. "Excellent. Now. Let's be more specific."

What in the world should she say? "It's none of your concern." That was true enough, just not good enough.

"It is when he's my customer. And it is when you're my supplier. And it especially is when you're having problems that affect my business."

Damn his logic. No matter which way she turned, he cornered her with another argument. He should have been that lower-than-low, slimier-than-slime, tackier-than-a-strip-of-flypaper lawyer, Thomas. Both men could take the sober truth and argue it into a drunken lie. What chance did she stand?

She pressed her lips together. Thor would have to put her on the rack before she'd admit to the outstanding loan her father left behind. Nor would she mention Jack Maxwell's offer. Not if she planned to live long enough to accept it.

"You were about to say?"

Andrea sighed. Racks be damned. She couldn't keep the truth from him forever. "All right. Joe and I were talking business. He'd come for an explanation about the poor quality of the produce. I told him what I told you."

"And he said?"

"Same as you said. Fix it."

"There's more. Spit it out."

How could he tell? she wondered in exasperation. This was downright unsettling. "I have bills from here into next Wednesday, and—" she slipped the last tidbit past him with casual indifference "—I'm seriously considering selling Constantine's."

"You're what!"

She was afraid he'd react that way. She cleared her throat. "I'm thinking of selling—"

"I heard what you said," he snapped. "I just don't believe it. Things can't be that bad." His mouth tightened. "Or is that an excuse? Do you want out of the business?"

"You're the genius. You go figure," she said, setting her chin at a stubborn angle.

"Okay. I will." His brows drew together as he mulled over the possibilities. "Perhaps you've been working at Constantine's all these years to satisfy your father. Now that he's gone, you can sell and enjoy the profits from his years of hard work. Is that it?"

Ironic amusement gleamed in her eyes. What profits? But if that was what he chose to think, she'd play along. "It's not like it's illegal or anything," she muttered, her gaze slipping away. "Isn't money to be enjoyed? Make hay while the sun shines and all that?"

He studied her, slowly shaking his head. "For some, but not for you. I know you too well to buy that one. I also know how hard you've worked to try and keep Constantine's going since your father's death. Nope, wrong answer. You don't have a mercenary bone in your body."

She glared at him indignantly. "I might..."

His lips twitched. "I think not. If you're selling, it's either because it's too much for you, or you think it's in the best interest of Constantine's."

"Now I'm a saint," she muttered.

He chuckled. "I wouldn't go that far. You're too proud for sainthood. And too stubborn." His penetrating gaze made her uncomfortable. "Somehow I don't think it's too much work. As I remember, you always thrived on that."

She strove for nonchalance. "If you say so."

"Which means you're selling because you believe it's in the best interest of Constantine's."

"Drop dead!"

"Bingo. So now we have the 'why' nailed. Next we work on the 'what if.'" He eyed her speculatively. "How about this one. If I could find a way to fix things so you didn't have to sell, what would you say to that?"

"'Thank you'?"

His hands dropped to her shoulders. "'Thank you'? That's it?"

She saw the trap and tried to tiptoe around it. "How about, 'What's in it for you?'"

"Smart question. Answer—protection of my markets."

"Is that all?"

"Retention of your Milano account."

Her smile held a touch of cynicism. "Anything else?"

He lowered his head close to her ear, and his warm breath brushed her cheek. "You."

She stepped away. "Forget it. I'm not part of the negotiations."

"Always so suspicious." His expression grew grim. "So wary of the ulterior motive."

"You taught me well."

"Wrong," he flashed back. "Your father taught you well. He's the one who always put Constantine's first, even ahead of his own daughter."

Her hands balled into fists. She wished she could deny his charge. It hurt that she couldn't. It hurt a lot. "Don't you say one more negative word about my father! If it hadn't been for him, you wouldn't be servicing the Milano account. You got a little greedy, is all."

He stepped closer. "Explain that remark!"

She refused to back down, refused to be intimidated by the fury glittering in his eyes. Instead she confronted him with a full year of pent-up resentment and anger. "I know about your attempt last year to get the Milanos to break their contract with Constantine's and go with you, instead. When that didn't work and you were forced to go through us, you saw me as the perfect tool. Our engagement ensured that Nick would give you the sweetest-possible deal."

A cool smile tugged at his lips. "You've forgotten one small detail. Business aside, I wanted you. I still do. I haven't figured out what terms it'll take to have you yet. But I will."

"No terms!" she whispered harshly. "I won't be a business pawn. Not again."

"We'll see." He crossed to the window and looked down at the loading dock. "Let's return to your problem. Right now the brokers and farmers who supply you see Constantine's as quick money. You're right. They don't respect you. You're a woman without protection. Easy prey."

"Rub it in," she groused. At the same time she felt relief that they were once again on a business footing. Business she could handle. It was touching she couldn't handle. Feeling. Anything that involved revealing her reaction to Thor's less-than-tender scrutiny.

"You also have competitors chipping away at your slice of the marketplace." He turned, stating baldly, "They're after *me* and my business, the biggest slice you own. And they'll do almost anything to get it."

She kept her expression blank. "Sounds like they're making you offers. Maybe you should consider one."

He shook his head. "You're right. I am greedy. I do want it all. I want a good deal on the produce I buy *and* I want the Milano account." He let that sink in before adding, "I also want you."

She glared at him. "We've been over that ground before. It's barren and won't be coming up daisies anytime in the near future."

"Won't it? You forget. The Thorsen name carries a lot of weight," he said in deliberate tones. "We command the respect you don't. Brokers wouldn't dare dump second-rate produce on me, nor would any of the farmers."

She shifted impatiently. "So, what do you propose? Are you going to personally call up all the brokers and farmers who supply me?"

"Yes."

"And tell them what?" she demanded. "That if they pull any more stunts with Andrea Constantine their corn is popped?"

He smiled. "Not quite. I'll tell them that if they pull any more stunts with Andrea *Thorsen* their corn is popped."

CHAPTER THREE

ANDREA STARED IN SHOCK. "You want me to marry you?"

"Got it in one."

"You're nuts!"

Thor laughed dryly. "I don't doubt it. Still, it'll solve your immediate problems, and mine, as well."

"And create a thousand new ones. You *can't* be serious." Panic crept into her voice. "I'll sell Constantine's. It's a much more reasonable solution than marriage."

"No, it isn't. According to our agreement, your selling means I'd forfeit the Milano account."

"Not necessarily. Not if the new owner chooses to keep it in force," Andrea protested.

She could convince Jack Maxwell to renew the Thorsen contract, couldn't she? She'd just have to point out all the advantages to him, explain the importance of maintaining it. He might service his restaurant business directly right now, but retaining the exclusive rights to the Thorsen markets was worth far more than the Milano account alone. Jack would understand. She'd *make* him understand.

Thor shook his head. "You can't guarantee that, can you?"

"No," she whispered reluctantly.

"The new owner might prefer to service Milano's Restaurants himself, and I wouldn't have a thing to say about it. I won't risk that happening. Not when I have an alternative. Besides, there's another reason why selling isn't a viable option."

She already knew it. By selling, far from living in the lap of luxury as he'd suggested, she'd be reduced to penury, all her profit going to the bank.

"Constantine's has dropped in value," she admitted. "I'm aware of that. It doesn't matter. I'm willing to take less."

He lifted an eyebrow. "You'd take less than half its former value? I'm surprised you're willing to give up so much."

The money didn't bother her. But Constantine's had been in the family for a long time. She hated to be the one to end it all. Nick hadn't intended to leave her swimming in debt, nor were the recent business problems his fault. They were hers. If he'd lived, he'd have found a way out of their troubles. By giving up, not only would she fail him and fail Constantine's, she'd fail herself.

"You've always accused me of having too much pride," she reminded Thor. "I'd think being forced to sell my business would provide me with a salutary lesson."

He nodded. "It would. Unfortunately it would also provide me with a salutary lesson. Something I'd prefer to do without. By marrying a Thorsen and restoring Constantine's clout, you'd be able to rebuild the business. I find that a much more profitable lesson. Don't you?"

Her mind raced. If he was right, if by marrying him she could rebuild Constantine's, she'd have a chance to pay off her debt to the bank. And if, in the final crunch, she was forced to sell, perhaps she could safeguard the Milano account for Thor. Constantine's would no longer be hers, true, but she'd have done her very best on all fronts.

And Thor? Innate honesty made her squirm. He'd be the one most at risk. He would put in his time and effort to help her business, only to risk losing it all in the end. Expedience came to the rescue, providing her with the perfect rationalization. If she couldn't meet her debts, she'd *have* to sell, and he'd be minus one account, regardless. This way, they all had a shot at winning.

She glanced at Thor. Maybe she could convince him to help without marriage. If he played tough with her suppliers, her quality would return. The Thorsens would be happy, the Milanos would be happy, and she'd be very happy. Thor would have accomplished his goal and need never be the wiser about her financial problems. It *could* happen that way. Right?

"Well?" His harsh voice broke into her sunny daydream. "What's your answer?"

"I don't know..." she said, temporizing.

His voice grew colder than she'd ever heard it. "Let me help you make up your mind. If you decide to sell, instead of marrying me, I'll break my contract with you and pull the Thorsen business. How much revenue would that cost you?"

She swallowed, her daydream firmly banished beneath a dark and threatening sky. "You know how much."

"Yes, I do. With all the trade your competitors have bled off, losing me on top of it would hurt, wouldn't it?" He stepped closer, his words sharp and merciless. "The produce business is a close-knit community. Within hours of our breaking the contract and going to one of your competitors, the news would be out. How many of your other customers will follow the Thorsen lead? And how will our desertion affect the sale of Constantine's?"

Her daydream turned into a nightmare. Jack wouldn't care if the Thorsens chose to buy elsewhere; he was after the Milano account. Unfortunately the severe drop in revenue might not give her enough time to complete the sale before going bankrupt. Jack was a nice guy, but business was business. If he heard of Constantine's financial difficulty, he might stall the sale until she went under. Then he could woo, and quite possibly win, the Milano account without it costing him a dime. She couldn't risk that happening.

She glared at Thor. "Damn you!"

"You did that a long time ago!"

"So it's revenge, is that it?"

"That's right. I play knight in shining armor, snatch your pretty backside from the fire, ensure you'll live in comfort for some time to come, and I'm doing it out of revenge."

"Then why?" she demanded in frustration.

"You figure it out. All I require is an answer."

"Just like that. Now?"

"I don't have a lot of time. My business is hurting, and since it's a family business, so's my family. I won't allow the situation to continue much longer. If you're going to sell, I want to know, so I can terminate our contract and cut my losses."

"Regardless of what it does to Constantine's?" she asked bitterly.

"You do have an alternative."

"If—" she chose her words with care "—if I agree to marry you, would it have to be permanent?"

"I'm not that altruistic." She winced, knowing she deserved the blunt statement. "After six months, maybe a year, we can divorce. You'd still have my name and the Thorsen protection. We'll make it clear it's an amicable parting. Your suppliers and competitors won't trouble you again. I'll see to that."

She looked away. He moved too fast. She didn't have a prayer of outthinking or outmaneuvering him. All she could do was stall. "I need time."

He cut her off at the pass. "I'll give you forty-eight hours. After that I'll assume you plan to sell. According to my contract I have to give seven days' written notice of my intent to terminate. Unless you agree to my suggestion, that notice will be on your desk first thing Wednesday morning."

Andrea bowed her head. "Why, Thor?" she whispered. "Why are you doing this?"

"You wouldn't believe me if I told you."

She gave a watery laugh. "Maybe it's something in the air. This is my second proposal today."

His voice remained even, though she suspected she'd angered him. "Mine's the better one. Marriage to Milano wouldn't work. He loves women too much to stay faithful to any one."

She couldn't disagree. "Ironic, isn't it?" She lifted her chin proudly. "No matter who I marry, I'll still end up divorced."

He gave no quarter. "Life's tough."

LATE THAT EVENING, Andrea climbed up the back warehouse steps to a tiny storage loft located above the offices. She leaned against the door, exhaustion sweeping over her. After Nick's death, she'd put their home on the market and sold most of its furnishings. Last week, the escrow closed and today she'd mailed the check from the proceeds to the bank in an attempt to lessen her debt. All that remained of the home she'd shared with her father for almost twenty-seven years were a few personal possessions she couldn't bear to part with, and a phone with her former number, which she didn't *dare* part with. Few people knew about the sale, but it would soon become public knowledge if anyone tried to call her at home and reached a disconnected number.

She unlocked the loft door and pushed it open. Home wasn't quite what it used to be, but it would do. It had taken a massive amount of cleaning and a lot of imagination to turn the dark tiny hole into a pleasant hideaway.

Switching on the overhead bulb, she stepped inside, welcomed by the glitter of hundreds of dancing prisms hanging from every conceivable fixture. Dodging the sparkling bits of glass, she hurried over to a small window and opened it. Seattle's hot July days left the loft of the cavernous old building stuffy. Fortunately, with only one room to cool, an electric fan solved the problem. Sort of.

In no time at all she'd boiled water for coffee on the little hot plate that served as a stove top. Eggs out of a miniature refrigerator followed, accompanied by a salad overflowing with assorted vegetables. She grinned. With a built-in produce market two floors below, at least she wouldn't starve.

The only drawback to her new accommodations was the necessity of going downstairs to use the bathroom and to refill her thermos jug whenever she needed water. But considering that she lived rent free, she couldn't complain. Besides it was temporary. As soon as she turned the business around...

"Ms. Constantine?" a voice called from the stairwell.

She opened the loft door and looked down into the anxious face of her night security guard. "Yes, Willie?"

"Thought I'd check to see if you're okay. I'll be outside for a while, if you need me. You, ah, sure you should stay here all by yourself?"

"I'm fine," she said firmly.

He cleared his throat. "I spoke to Marco today."

Andrea winced, wondering if Willie had let anything slip about her new residence. Except for the guard, no one knew she'd moved into the warehouse. And she preferred to keep it that way. For some reason, her employees had become very protective of late. If they found out she was living in the loft, not only would they worry about her safety—not that there was anything to worry *about*—they'd also wonder why she'd sold her home. She couldn't afford to start rumors concerning Constantine's financial position. Not now. Not ever.

"What did you tell Marco?" she asked.

"Nothing!" he was quick to claim. "Not a word, just like I promised. Only..."

"Only?"

He yanked at the brim of his hat. "Marco's my cousin, you see."

Andrea closed her eyes and counted to ten. It didn't help. "I'm sorry," she said carefully. "I realize the uncomfortable position that puts you in, but I'd appreciate your continued discretion."

"Sure thing. It's just..."

"Yes?"

"Watching over a few bananas and apples isn't no big deal." He tugged significantly at his belt, his sidearm bouncing against his thigh. "A crazed desperado puts a few bullet holes in a bag of spuds, and you can up and buy some more. But I'd feel real bad if you were to...ah..." He shrugged. "You know."

"Become bullet-ridden while in your care?"

"Yeah." He sighed in relief. "I'd feel real bad if that happened. It could cause big trouble for both of us. Major big trouble. And..."

"Yes, Willie?"

He stared up at her earnestly, his devoted puppy-dog face beaded with perspiration. "This is temporary, like you promised, isn't it Ms. Constantine?"

"Of course it is." She smiled, positive all her woes could be dealt with before too many months passed. "And I'll do my very best not to get shot up. All right?"

"I guess that'll have to do," he agreed unhappily. He began to retreat down the steps. "You'll remember to bar your door?"

"I'll remember, Willie."

He paused at the landing. "And keep that crowbar I gave you real handy. Under your pillow, okay?"

"I will." She choked on the lie. Not even for Willie's peace of mind would she sleep on top of a lump of iron.

"And call me if you hear anything peculiar." He disappeared around the landing, then peeked back at her. "Anything at all."

"You'll be the first to know." He vanished again and she stepped into the loft.

"'Night, Ms. Constantine," came the faint farewell. "Sleep tight."

"Good night, Willie," she replied, and started to close her door.

His mournful voice drifted up with a final admonishment. "Don't let the bedbugs bite."

ANDREA AWOKE the next morning to a room flooded with rainbows. Sunshine, streaming in from the skylights above her bed and from the tiny porthole windows along one wall, caught each of the hundreds of prisms and filled her room with the promise of a better tomorrow. At least, that was how she'd always attributed the gift the prisms offered.

She sat up and wrapped her arms around her bent legs, gazing at the sparkling bits of glass suspended amongst the dust motes. So pretty and simple, yet add a little light and look at what they could accomplish. A rainbow and a miracle, all in one.

It also expressed her philosophy about life.

The rainbows gave her hope and reinforced her belief that everything, no matter how impossible it seemed at the mo-

ment, would work out in the end. It might take a little time
and imagination, and it might also take a heck of a lot of
effort, but eventually all her problems could be happily resolved. Faith, like sunlight on a prism, was the magical ingredient.

Unfortunately realism was an ingredient, as well. And a
roomful of rainbows meant she'd overslept. Hopping off the
bed, she threw on her clothes. With any luck, she could still
slip down to her office with no one any the wiser....

Except for Marco, the ten salesmen and dozen or so dock
workers who'd been searching for her all morning.

"You had to be somewhere. Your car's parked in the lot,"
Marco groused when she made her appearance. "Where you
been hiding?"

"The loft," she admitted, honest to a fault. "Looking at
prisms."

"You gone daft on me?" Marco demanded. "Can't work
for no daft-minded boss."

She glared at him, not that it helped. A fair number of the
men in her employ had known her since she was in diapers.
One or two, she didn't doubt, had even changed the occasional soggy drawer. Which gave her more substitute fathers
than she cared to count, each more protective than the last.

"Every marble present and accounted for," she assured
him. "What's the problem?"

"We've got a boycott in the making," he said, not pulling any punches.

Andrea closed her eyes. Hartsworth and his scum-of-the-
earth lawyer, Thomas. What she wouldn't give to lock them
both up for a week with some of that worm-ridden, rot-
infested corn they'd tried to pawn off on her. "Go on. I can
take it." Maybe she could take it. She'd try to take it.

"Three phone calls so far. Each from farmers out of
eastern Washington, same as Hartsworth, with every last

son-of-a-hee-haw yammering on about our history of non-payment." He scowled. "They're all demanding cash in hand *before* delivery."

"Right. Then *if* they deliver, it won't be fit for pig slop." Not to mention the fact their current problems stemmed from just that sort of arrangement. The last time Nick paid in advance, the farming co-op he'd fronted went belly-up, adding to their financial hole. A hole fast approaching the size of the Grand Canyon. "Forget it."

Marco hesitated, his expression reflecting his frustration. "I'm not sure we have a choice," he muttered. "I wish I could call up every last one of those yahoos and give 'em what for. But we need their produce. Without it . . ." His shrug spoke volumes. "Our inventory won't last forever."

"We could buy elsewhere."

"Not according to the brokers I've approached," he informed her tartly. "Seems your friend Hartsworth's got us wrapped up tighter than a sex-starved boa would its mate."

She whistled softly. "I assume that's tight."

"Count on it."

She could also count on Constantine's being in an even tougher position, if that was possible, should she agree to their terms. "Okay, what do we do?"

"You're the boss. It's your call."

"I'll talk to them personally. Maybe it'll help. How long can we get by?"

"Two days. Oh, and young Milano was here. Said he'd call you later."

Andrea nodded. She didn't have time to worry about Joe. Staying in business came first. She walked into her office and picked up the phone, aware that a solution to her predicament did exist—for the truly desperate. Which she wasn't. At least, not yet. With luck, not ever.

Six hours later her luck ran out. Not only did she learn the meaning of the word "desperate," she'd learned the meaning of the words "pure" "unadulterated" and "panic." She unglued her ear from the phone and, in one furious move, swept her desk clean. Receipts, envelopes and bills formed a colorful barrier around her desk.

Each of the men she'd spoken to was more stubborn than the most ornery mule, and twice as contrary. If she wanted any more deliveries she either paid for them in advance and in cash, or she scuttled over to Thorsen's Produce, tail tucked firmly between legs, and dumped her problems in Thor's lap. Neither was a prospect she relished.

She thrust her chair aside and stood, stalking to the windows overlooking the warehouse. All her life she'd lived with a man who'd put business first—even, as Thor had so kindly reminded her, before his only child. Not that Nick hadn't been a loving father. But it had hurt, knowing she'd always come second in his life.

When she'd discovered she couldn't successfully compete with the demands of Constantine's, she'd tried to work for him and prove her worth that way, share with him on a level he'd understand. Not that it had done much good. Nick didn't approve of women in the business, a business that occupied all his time and energy. So, long ago she'd decided never to marry a man who felt the same way.

Until she'd met Thor, who'd promptly blown that decision to hell and gone. Still, she'd hoped. She'd hoped that she'd fallen in love with a different type of man than Nick. Hoped Thor loved her even a smidgen more than his business. Hoped, for once, she could be first in someone's life.

The truth, when it came, had been painful, if not unforeseen. Shortly after their engagement, she'd discovered Thor had proposed only to get the best possible deal from Nick during negotiations for the Milano account. She'd returned his ring.

How ironic that she'd come full circle, agreeing to marry a man who chose business over love. How the mighty did fall. She closed her eyes. And how Thor must be laughing.

With an effort, she straightened her shoulders. Maybe she could still have the last laugh. By marrying, she could save Constantine's and pay off the bank. She'd succeed where once she was doomed to fail. Yes. She'd do it. She'd play Thor at his own game. And win.

Now to beard the thunder god in his den.

AT NINE THAT NIGHT darkness enshrouded the inside of Thorsen's main store in downtown Seattle. The two floors above the market also appeared deserted, all except for a single light on the upper level shining from the window of a corner office. Thor's office.

A night watchman let Andrea in, and she reached the top floor, struggling to catch her breath. Climbing two flights of stairs wouldn't normally leave her winded, not with her life-style. Nor would it make her heart pound so erratically. She ran a hand through her short curls, groaning in dismay to discover her fingers shook. Pitiful. Absolutely pitiful.

Okay, so she was scared. It wasn't a sin, for crying out loud. Any woman about to throw herself at a man's feet, prostrate herself before him, plead for mercy, would be just as scared.

She paused, chewing on her lip. Maybe she wouldn't have to plead. These things weren't mandatory, after all. She brightened. Of course not. She could leave out that part. He'd never miss it. With any luck she could skip over the prostrating bit, too. And instead of throwing, perhaps she could toss herself at him. Gently.

That resolved, she found the nerve to walk down the long hallway to his office. His door stood open. He sat behind his desk, his tawny head bent over some papers. Her nerve cut and ran. Deciding to follow suit, she reversed engines, determined to beat a hasty retreat. She couldn't cope with this right now.

"Andrea?"

Too late. "You're busy. I'll come another time," she called, backpedaling down the hall and nearly tripping over her own two feet.

He appeared in the doorway, leaning against the jamb. A lazy grin spread across his broad mouth. "Chicken," he murmured in a husky voice.

She nodded. "Cluck. Cluck."

He held out a hand. "Come on, sweetheart. You got this far. You might as well finish it."

His hand was large and strong, heavy calluses ridging his palm and fingers. She took a deep breath and slowly, tentatively, with utmost caution, returned to his side and fit her hand into his. The soothing warmth of his fingers engulfed her and she relaxed, her resistance fading. Her hand felt at home.

He tugged her closer, so close, in fact, that if she inched forward just a tad, she'd be in his arms. She'd missed those arms about her, their tender power, their warmth and security. She'd also missed the way their bodies fit in such perfect alignment, his height easily topping her extra inches.

"So," he rumbled close to her ear, laughter evident in his deep tones, "to what do I owe the honor?"

She sighed, giving in. Maybe pleading, prostrating and throwing herself at his feet wouldn't be so bad, after all. Which, she wondered, would he expect first? Pleading, most likely.

"I've come to pl—" She lifted a hand to her throat, choking on the word.

He chuckled. "Pl? Pl what?"

"Pl—" The word refused to leave her tongue. She tried to scrape it off with her teeth and came up empty. Maybe prostrating would work better. "I've come to pros—"

"Pl pros?" His mouth twitched. "Is that a new fruit, perhaps? Put me down for five cases."

She took a steadying breath. The man redefined insufferable! He knew full well why she'd come. Why didn't he help a little?

"I've come..." Her chin shot up. The hell with it. "I've come for proof." Yeah, proof. That beat out plead and prostrate any day of the week, not to mention tossing herself at his feet. "You said you could help solve my problems if I'd marry you. I'll agree to marriage *if* you show me some proof first." She groaned. No question about it. Her pride was fully present and accounted for, every last bit of it.

His smile turned sardonic. "Of course. Pl pros. Proof. I don't know why I didn't make the connection right away." She was obliged to agonize through a full two minutes of uncomfortable silence. Just when she'd reached the breaking point and was ready to cave in, he said, "Tell me your problem. I'll take care of it. My pleasure."

A grub couldn't have felt lower than she did at that moment. She crossed to the chair in front of his desk and perched on the edge. In a minimum of words, she filled in the gaps about the situation with Hartsworth, Thomas and the eastern Washington farmers.

"I realize there isn't much you can do tonight," she concluded.

"No?" He flipped through his personal directory and picked up the phone, punching in a series of numbers. "Oh, ye of little faith. Listen and learn."

He called his own lawyer first. After giving the attorney a specific list of instructions, he phoned Mr. Thomas. She didn't have the nerve to ask where Thor had gotten the man's home number, and on such short notice, too. Or had he anticipated her coming to him? Considering his ultimatum, her arrival couldn't have been much of a surprise.

"This is Thor Thorsen," he announced briskly, listening for a moment before replying, "That's right. Thorsen's Produce. I understand there's some conflict between your client, Mr. Hartsworth, and my fiancée, Andrea Constantine." He fell silent for several moments more. "That's an interesting claim, though not quite what the federal produce inspectors state on their report. I've instructed my attorney to file suit against Mr. Hartsworth on behalf of Ms. Constantine first thing in the morning."

He lifted his foot and rested it on the desk, dangling the phone from its cord. He smiled at Andrea. It took five minutes before the voice shrieking through the receiver quieted.

Thor spoke again. "No, you listen to me. This is my one and only offer. Your client will have a truckload of corn sitting on Constantine's loading dock within twenty-four hours. Once that's done, a certified check will be messengered to Mr. Hartsworth. What's your answer?" He smiled. "I thought so. Nice doing business with you."

"That's it?" she demanded, watching as he hung up. "Thomas agreed?"

"Of course."

Of course. She sat and stewed. He resolved her problem with such ease. Why did she find that so annoying? She knew why. Because she couldn't handle it on her own. All her pleading and all her threats hadn't done a bit of good. But one word from Thor Thorsen and people fell all over themselves to do his bidding. Corn would magically appear on her dock. The farmers would fight to be the first to deliver their apples. Undoubtedly quality would improve a thousandfold. The scenario left a bitter taste in her mouth.

"You don't seem pleased," he observed.

"I'm not," she admitted with blunt honesty. "I'm grateful, but I'm not pleased. It shouldn't require male interference to take care of Constantine's problems."

"No, it shouldn't. If it bothers you so much, get out of the business."

Her eyes flashed with anger. "I can't, remember? If I try to sell Constantine's, you'll dump me. The business could fold."

He shrugged. "The way things are going, it'll fold, anyway."

"No, it won't!"

"Face facts. You can't win on your own." He leaned across the desk, his facade of indifference disappearing. "You've always loved working the business. Are you going to let a bunch of unscrupulous bastards force you out? They fight by fair means or foul. Take a leaf from their book. If you use their own rules against them, you stand a chance of winning."

She looked away, her spine rigid with defiance. She'd told Thor that if he solved her problem with Hartsworth, she'd marry him. It was a promise she'd honor just as she honored all her business commitments. But first, they'd discuss the terms of surrender.

Her mouth turned down. "All right. I need you. There, I've admitted it."

"That's big of you," he said dryly.

"Do you still insist on marriage?"

"I do."

"Do you object to a prenuptial agreement keeping our two businesses separate?"

"No. I prefer it."

"Okay. I'll marry you." She glanced at him, and froze in her chair. Triumph glowed deep in his eyes, turning the color a brilliant sea blue. So he'd beaten her, after all. He must be very pleased. Foreboding filled her, teasing her with what lay ahead—a marriage based on desire and business, not on love.

"About time," he muttered in a rough voice. He stood and she followed suit, backing away.

"I want a few marital ground rules set up first," she spoke hastily.

He smiled and his resemblance to a huge hungry lion grew. "Such as?"

"We divorce in three months."

He shook his head and came around the side of his desk. "Six. Minimum. It'll take at least that long to get Constantine's shaped up."

"Okay, six," she agreed, edging away. "But I can't marry you for two more months. Things are too hectic at work right now."

"We marry in four weeks."

She put the chair between them. "That's too soon!"

"Tough."

"The wedding," she gasped, as he hooked a foot around the chair leg and booted it to one side. "It's to be small and intimate."

"Try large and public and at my church." He kept coming. "The whole purpose of this ceremony is to broadcast it to as many people as possible, not keep it quiet. I'll take care of the wedding arrangements. All you have to do is show up. Any more conditions I should know about?"

"Yes! I...I won't share a home with you." She took several quick steps backward. "There's no reason to. It isn't like this is a real marriage or anything."

He grinned in amusement. "I think we'll leave that question open for future negotiation. Anything else?"

She nodded, speaking fast, aware she'd soon run out of retreating room. "And I won't have...be..." Her eyes widened in alarm as he reached her. "No touching!"

"Trust me. There will be lots of touching. Starting now."

The bright glitter from his hammer earring flashed like a warning beacon before his gentle yank sent her tumbling into his arms. He slid one hand around her waist, the other up her spine to the nape of her neck. His fingers eased into her hair, becoming entangled in her short blond curls. He studied her upturned face, his expression serious, almost thoughtful.

"I've waited a long time for this," he murmured, and lowered his mouth to hers.

She stiffened against him, part of her desperate to fight him off. The other, more insidious part wallowed in the mind-splintering sensations he aroused. She'd forgotten— heavens, how'd she'd forgotten!—the impact of his kiss. It was like soaring over one of her rainbows straight into a miracle. Hope and faith and promises abounded.

It was impossible to resist. With a tiny sigh, she relaxed, taking the momentary joy offered. She'd worry about the consequences later. Much later.

"There's your touching rule taken care of," he muttered against her mouth, satisfaction heavy in his voice. "Shall we lay odds on how long we maintain separate living accommodations?"

CHAPTER FOUR

LATER THAT NIGHT, Andrea stood in the middle of her loft and silently fumed. How could she have forgotten, even for a single instant, what a total louse her ex-fiancé—correction, *current* fiancé—was?

Her brow puckered in a brooding frown, and she ran a hand over a cluster of prisms, sending them spinning. How many of her ground rules had he swept aside? All but one by her reckoning, and then only because he'd chosen not to fight over maintaining separate living accommodations. Yet. Would she have any luck holding him off if he made an issue of it? She hadn't with any of her other demands.

He'd summarily dismissed her proposed limit of a three-month marriage. She grimaced. Okay, so he'd come up with a reasonable excuse. That didn't mean he could dictate how they'd marry, when they'd marry and even where they'd marry.

Although, loath as she was to admit it, a large wedding did make good business sense. And if they *had* to wed, the sooner they got it over with the better. As to the rest of the wedding arrangements, she didn't really mind his taking care of those.

But his audacity in breaking that touching rule . . .

She shivered. He'd leveled her with his kiss, no doubt about it. He'd taken her emotions and turned them upside down, inside out and all-around backward. How could she have let that happen? And how could she protect herself in the future?

No touching, that was how, she vowed then and there. Certainly no kissing. Not even a friendly hug. Before he said, "I do," he'd have to promise, "I won't"!

Much relieved at her taking a hand in her own fate, she climbed into bed and snuggled beneath the covers. One final annoying question popped into her head. Why, she wondered, vaguely insulted, hadn't he insisted they live together? Her lower lip inched out as sleep laid claim. *You'd think he'd have insisted.*

THE NEXT TWO WEEKS flew by, bringing her wedding day closer and closer, and stretching her nerves further and further. She didn't hear a word from Joe Milano, much to her relief. Either he didn't know about her forthcoming nuptials—an unlikely possibility, considering the size of the announcement Thor put in the newspaper—or he thought discretion the better part of valor.

She grinned, flipping through the pile of papers cluttering her desk. It probably wasn't either of those. At a guess, Caesar had ordered him to stay away. After all, Joe could take full credit for breaking up her engagement last time. Caesar might be unwilling to risk that happening again.

The phone rang from somewhere nearby. Four rings later she uncovered it beneath a stack of produce brochures. "Constantine's," she said hurriedly into the receiver.

"Andrea?" a lightly accented voice responded. "Sonja Thorsen here."

"Hello, Mrs. Thorsen." Andrea tensed. Why in the world would Thor's mother be calling?

"Make it 'Sonja,' please. I'd like to discuss wedding plans with you, if it's convenient."

Andrea sagged in relief. Naturally. How silly not to realize right off. "Wedding plans. Of course. I'd forgotten." She bit her tongue. Not the most diplomatic thing to admit to her future mother-in-law. Her *temporary* future mother-in-law, she corrected.

Sonja chuckled. "I'm surprised you're so calm, considering all Thor's plans for this ceremony."

Say what? Andrea straightened in her chair. "Pardon?"

"I'm pleased you trust me with the wedding preparations. But I'm uncertain about one or two of the details. Would you have time to get together for lunch tomorrow? I realize how busy you are at Constantine's..."

Tomorrow. Tomorrow. Where had she put her calendar book? Andrea shuffled through her papers. *Think, damn it.* She'd last seen it beneath the phone messages. No, she vaguely remembered burying it under last quarter's profit-and-loss statement.

Misinterpreting the prolonged silence, Sonja added hesitantly. "It won't be the two of us alone. Jordan will be there. I thought you'd appreciate her involvement."

"Thank you, I would. If I seem a little disorganized, it's because I'm a little disorganized."

Sonja laughed, her relief clear. "I've never known a bride who wasn't."

Finding her book, Andrea hastily flipped through the pages. Anything scheduled could be canceled. "Tomorrow? Looks fine," she assured Sonja. Taking an extraordinary amount of satisfaction, she drew a heavy black line through Thor's noon appointment. "What time would work best for you?"

"Does one o'clock suit?"

"One's perfect."

"Good." There was a delicate pause. Then the older woman said, "I'm delighted you and Thor are together again. I never met such a well-suited couple."

Oh, Lord. What did she say to that? "I—you—he—" *Clever, Andrea. Very articulate.* She sighed, giving up. "Thanks."

"I've embarrassed you, haven't I? I'm sorry," Sonja said, then added briskly, "You must be busy, so I won't keep you. I look forward to tomorrow. We'll talk then. *Adjø, datter.*"

Goodbye, daughter. It had a pleasant ring to it. "'Bye," Andrea murmured, and hung up.

She stared at the phone for several long seconds, something the other woman said nagging at her. What did she mean, *all* Thor's plans for their wedding ceremony? *All* made things sound rather elaborate. He'd promised to take care of the wedding arrangements. Just what, she wondered in growing suspicion, did that entail? Snatching up the receiver, she started dialing.

She ignored Thor's friendly greeting. "What's going on?" she demanded abruptly.

"Skip your morning coffee, sweetheart?"

"Don't sweetheart me. I just spoke to your mother, and she's acting like our marriage is going to be real or something."

"It will be real. Very real."

"You know what I mean," she snarled into the receiver. "Sonja's invited me to lunch tomorrow."

"No! How could she do that to her future daughter-in-law?"

"Stop laughing and be serious! Did you warn her about the divorce?"

"I just told her about the wedding. It seemed a little crass to talk divorce so soon after announcing our engagement."

She ground her teeth. "I want you to tell your family the truth."

"And what is the truth?"

"That we're marrying to protect our joint business interests."

"No, that's why *you're* marrying."

His statement stopped her cold. What did he mean by that? "What do you mean by that? If it isn't for business reasons, why are you marrying me?"

"Still haven't figured it out?"

"Apparently not. Care to clue me in?"

He chuckled. "Nope. And as for your request, I have no intention of mentioning a divorce to my family. You, on the other hand, may feel free to tell them anything you'd like."

"You don't mind?" she asked, nonplussed.

"If I did, I wouldn't have suggested it. I'm not reticent about my wishes, now am I?"

"No, you're not." Anything but. Not only wasn't he reticent, he also had a very effective method of getting her to go along with him. She touched her lips, remembering. Too effective.

"Andrea?"

"What?"

"Is there anything else? I do have business to take care of."

His words stung and she didn't like it. He shouldn't have that power over her any longer. "There's nothing else," she said shortly, and hung up.

Fifteen seconds later the phone rang. She answered it automatically. "Constant—"

"You didn't say goodbye," Thor's voice rumbled against her ear. "I'm not so busy I don't have time to say a proper goodbye to my fiancée."

A tiny smile flickered across her mouth. The idiot. "Goodbye, Mr. Thorsen."

"If I were there, I'd be touching you." At her soft gasp, he murmured, "Goodbye, sweetheart."

Before she could gather her wits sufficiently to respond, he hung up. Warm color crept into her cheeks as she slowly replaced the receiver. Not again. She couldn't let herself feel anything for him again. It hurt too much. She shut her eyes and groaned. To her dismay, she realized that decision had come much, much too late.

THE NEXT DAY at precisely one o'clock, Andrea pulled into the Thorsens' driveway. The few times she'd visited during her previous engagement to Thor, she'd been enchanted by the sprawling estate. Perched high atop the hillside of Magnolia, it commanded a magnificent view of Puget Sound.

Stepping from her car, she paused to watch the ferries move across the steel-gray waters. She wished she could stand here all day taking in the glory of the Olympic Mountains and the crisp refreshing scent of the salty air. But she couldn't. Unable to delay the inevitable, she crossed the broad expanse of green lawn. Jordan Roberts, now Thorsen, sat in a swing on the front porch.

"I was too excited to wait inside," the petite brunette admitted. She gave a gaminelike grin. "I'm thrilled for you and Thor. I never thought you'd make up. Tell me everything."

Guilt swept over Andrea. She should have called and explained the true circumstances surrounding her wedding. The two of them had been best friends all their lives, partially due to the fact that Jordan's family owned a retail produce market. For as many years as Andrea could remember, the Roberts and the Constantines had done business together. It wasn't until the Thorsens had bought

Cornucopia, Jordan's market, and she'd married Thor's brother, that a certain reserve had grown between them. *Be honest,* she commanded herself silently. *You've felt reserved, not Jordan.*

Andrea cleared her throat, determined to confess all. "Yes, well—"

Jordan jumped up and gave her an impulsive hug, the bulge of her stomach butting against Andrea's hip. "Look at how huge I've gotten," she said, patting the protrusion. "It's all Rainer's fault."

Andrea lifted an eyebrow. "I'm relieved to hear it."

"I meant," Jordan said with a groan, "that the Thorsens are big men. They grow big babies. I guess you'll find that out soon enough." She grinned slyly. "Oh-ho, that made you blush."

"About this wedding—"

"We'll have plenty of time to discuss it after lunch." Jordan linked her arm with Andrea's and ushered her in the door. "You should see the spread Sonja prepared."

"I can't wait, but—"

"Alaric's looking forward to seeing you, too. I always suspected he had a soft spot where you were concerned."

Andrea hadn't expected to see Thor's father, so the news came as a pleasant surprise. "He's a sweetie," she agreed, thinking fast. Maybe she wouldn't say anything about the divorce. There'd be plenty of time to confess the truth later. Why rush in and ruin things? Yes, she'd wait until a more appropriate time.

To Andrea's relief, lunch progressed very pleasantly. She'd forgotten how much she liked Thor's mother. The tall slender woman had a delightful sense of humor, her hazel eyes constantly alight with mischief. And Alaric, with his droll wit, kept them all laughing straight through the final cup of coffee.

Once they were finished, Sonja stood. "This has been wonderful," she declared. "But if you'll excuse me, I'll take care of these dishes. Jordan, why don't you help me." She waved a restraining hand at Andrea. "No, no. You sit. We won't be a minute."

Alaric waited until the two women left before speaking. "So Thor finally managed to hook you again," he commented in his blunt fashion. "I didn't think he'd pull it off."

She smiled, reluctant to bring up uncomfortable topics. "I didn't make it easy for him."

"Good." He nodded his approval. "He'll value winning you all the more." He thumped the arms of his wheelchair. "If it weren't for this thing, I'd have given him a fine swift kick when he first lost you."

"Would it have worked?" she asked, her smile growing.

He returned her grin with one so much like Thor's it hurt. "Not with him. He's stubborn."

"Really?" she murmured. "I hadn't noticed." An instant later they both broke into laughter.

"You will be good for my son," Alaric approved. "He needs someone with a sense of humor."

"I agree," Sonja said, breezing into the room with Jordan. She stopped by Alaric's chair and gave his shoulder a loving squeeze. "The sooner they marry, the better. For now, come. I have a surprise for you, Andrea. Jordan, you should see this, as well."

She led them upstairs and down a hallway. Opening the door to a guest room, she gestured at the bed. Spread out on the quilted coverlet lay a beautiful Norwegian dress. An apron embroidered in red, white, green and gold covered the forest-green, calf-length skirt. Matching embroidery decorated the collar of the white blouse and trim of the red vest. Andrea ran a gentle hand over the silver filigree buttons edging the bodice.

"This is lovely!" she exclaimed.

"It's a *bunad*." Sonja smiled, misty-eyed. "Three generations of women in my family have been married in this gown. I'd be honored if you wore it on your wedding day, Andrea."

"I couldn't!" She spoke without thought, and then glanced apprehensively at the older woman, unable to hide her dismay. It would be a mockery for her to wear something with such a rich tradition. But how could she explain that to Thor's mother? "You . . . you're too generous," she said weakly.

"Nonsense. It's a wonderful idea," Jordan said with an excited laugh. "I was too short to wear it for my wedding. This will be the perfect alternative. Won't Thor be surprised when he sees you?"

That could possibly be the understatement of the century. "I don't think—" Andrea began.

"You have to have a *bunad*," Jordan interrupted. "It's a traditional wedding. That means wearing a traditional gown."

Andrea strove to appear less confused than she felt. "Traditional?"

"Jordan's right. It would seem strange if the bride wore anything else. I'm sure Thor expects it," Sonja concurred. "Besides, it would mean so much to me."

And that said it all. What else could she do but give in? "I'd love to, thank you," she said sincerely, and gave her mother-in-law-to-be a quick hug. "That takes care of the dress. What's left?"

Jordan's eyes gleamed with laughter. "Horseback lessons, for one. Do you know how to ride sidesaddle?"

Andrea blinked. "We're getting married on a horse?"

"Thor didn't tell you, did he?" Sonja sighed, muttering something rude in Norwegian. At least Andrea assumed it was rude. It certainly sounded rude.

She fought down panic. "Tell me what?"

The other two exchanged significant glances. Sonja enlightened her. "That it's to be a traditional Norwegian country wedding," she said. "Thor's insisted on it all—authentic costumes, a three-day celebration, a horseback wedding procession to the church."

"I think he overlooked mentioning that little detail," Andrea admitted numbly. And when she got her hands on that man, he wouldn't walk for a week, much less ride a damn horse to his—*their* wedding.

"Honestly! What could he be thinking of?" his mother fumed.

"That she'd bolt if he told her," Andrea's best friend in the whole world blithely revealed. "Which she would. Except we won't let her."

"Thanks," Andrea muttered. "You're a real pal."

Jordan's voice turned coaxing. "But it'll be such fun. I've never been to a country wedding before, and Rainer says they're spectacular. Each one's a little different, depending on which part of Norway you come from."

"I'm sure Thor wants the wedding to be an occasion you'll remember for the rest of your life," Sonja suggested. "An event your grandchildren will talk about."

"But...you don't understand." Tears filled Andrea's dark eyes and she blinked rapidly. Why had Thor done this to her? Didn't he realize it put her in a very awkward position? "Ours isn't going to be a real marriage," she confessed, her voice trembling despite her best attempts to keep it even. "It's...it's a business relationship."

"Right. Pull the other one," Jordan said with a snort, then studied her friend more closely. "You're serious!"

"We have to have a big wedding so everyone will hear of it," Andrea revealed. Her explanation sounded strange even to her. She tried again. "That way my competitors will leave us, Constantine's, that is, alone. It's temporary, you see. We don't *love* each other or anything."

"Bridal nerves," Sonja and Jordan proclaimed in unison, and burst out laughing.

"It's not! It's business."

"Very practical." Sonja approved. "Love has a nasty way of clouding the issue. Though I wouldn't be a bit surprised if you don't find lots of—" she hesitated, smiling "—*practical* reasons to stay together."

"But not love," Jordan was quick to insert. "That's too *im*practical."

Andrea gave up. What was the point? They'd believe what they chose. And they chose not to believe her reasons for marrying Thor. It didn't matter. Let them keep their illusions as long as possible. They'd be shattered soon enough.

"I don't know what to say," she whispered.

"Don't say a thing." Sonja dropped an affectionate arm around her shoulders. "We'll take care of everything for you. Why don't we go over the arrangements so you know exactly what's going on? Don't worry. We'll all help you."

Feeling like the biggest fraud who ever walked, Andrea went along with them. But her bewilderment grew. Why was Thor going to all this trouble? It didn't make the least bit of sense.

TWO DAYS BEFORE the wedding, Joe came to Andrea's office for another visit. One look and she realized he'd worked himself into a fine rip-roaring temper.

"This you send to us and I bring back," he announced, tossing an envelope onto her desk.

She snatched it up, afraid it would sift through the layers of paper, never to be seen again. "What is it?"

"It is *money,*" he said in an offended tone. "How you do this, huh?"

"Do what?" She stared at him in bewilderment. "I owe you for that bad produce."

"I know you do not mean to insult us. But you do. To send this money, it is not right." He dropped into the chair in front of her desk and glowered.

"Of course it's right. It's done all the time."

He eyed her with suspicion. "I do not understand. Explain to me, please."

She leaned across the desk. "It's easy," she began in a confidential tone. "See, you get bad produce and call up Thor, complaining like the devil. Right?"

He cleared his throat. "To be honest, *cara,* I leave this complaining to my poppa."

"Yes. Well." She bit down on her lip. Hard. "*Caesar* calls and complains. Which makes Thor feel lower than dirt, and he refunds your money."

"Yes, it happen this way once or twice," he admitted.

"And why does Thor offer you a refund?" She answered her own question. "Because he wants to keep you happy and make lots of money off you later."

Joe glanced longingly at the envelope. "I think I understand. But Poppa, he only complains a little to Thorsen. We complain most to you."

"I know. But if you *had* complained a lot to Thor, he'd have called me up and screamed like, er, complained even louder. I'd have felt like pond scum and would've paid him off in order to shut him up."

"All this mud and pond skummings sounds very messy." He looked hopeful. "You are sure this is how it works?"

"Positive. All I've done is cut out the middleman. You know, the dirt and scum stuff." She grinned in triumph.

"Yes, I see. But..."

She could sense his opposition weakening. "Did you use the produce or throw it away?"

He shrugged. "I regret to say, we throw it out."

"Was it your fault?"

"No, no. The produce, it was bad."

"If you'd like, I can have you call and yell at Thor." She tried to appear duly chastened. "But then he'd have to phone back and treat me like slime."

"Not scum?"

"Okay, like scum. Do you want him to do that? In a few more days I'll be married to the guy."

It took Joe a full five seconds to reach a decision. "No, no. We take the money, so you do not be pond scum on your wedding day." He beamed and twitched the envelope from her fingers. Crossing to her side, he perched on the edge of the desk. "I am glad we settle this. We do good together. Why you not marry me, instead of Thorsen, huh?"

Andrea's tone was caustic. "We'd be at each other's throats before the honeymoon ended."

He sighed gustily. "But it would be a very good honeymoon."

"Did you have something else to discuss?" she asked, firmly steering him to the business at hand.

He pinched two fingers together. "Er, one teeny bitsy little thing more."

Uh-oh. "Yes?"

"I like to apologize for making you break it up with Thorsen last time. My words do this and I feel very bad." He peeked quickly round and, apparently satisfied, lowered his voice. "He heard what I say?"

She struggled to keep any hint of laughter from her voice. "Not from me. I haven't mentioned it."

"Good. I think if he knows, it is bye-bye baby for me. You promise to keep all the lips glued? In fact, you do not have to tell him I come here at all."

His expression was so pathetic she couldn't help but agree. "I promise. My lips are sealed."

He shook his head. "I feel very bad, *cara*. Thorsen will be your husband, and a wife should not keep secrets from her husband. But I am glad you do not tell him—"

"Not tell me what?" Thor stood in the open doorway. He nailed them with a furious look and strode into the room.

Joe leapt off her desk. "Very good to talk to you, *cara*. You have a good marriage. I see you soon." At Thor's thunderous glare, he added hastily. "No, no. I mean I see you not so soon. Maybe never again. I leave now, okay?" He edged around Thor.

"Okay by me," Thor agreed. He kicked the door shut behind Joe's retreating back and turned on Andrea.

She broke into speech as he approached. "Don't bother bellowing. It won't work."

"What aren't you supposed to tell me about?" he demanded, quieting his voice to just beneath a bellow.

He towered above the desk, putting her at an instant disadvantage. She wanted to answer him, but because of her promise to Joe, she couldn't. Nor could she lie. She despised lies; lies were wrong and they were always uncovered.

Except, with any luck, this one.

"He didn't want you to know about his visit." That wasn't a complete falsehood. Perhaps she could tell him certain truths, without telling him *the* truth. It would sure go a long way toward salving her conscience. Well, maybe a short way.

"Why not?"

She squirmed. Tough question and no answer. "Why do you think?" she countered.

"Because he loused up our engagement last time," Thor responded promptly, "and he knew I'd kill him if he did it again."

Andrea sat and blinked. So he knew. Unfortunate for Joe, but very fortunate for her. She peeked up at him and winced. Sort of. Perhaps an explanation was in order. "When Joe filled me in on the details about the Milano deal last year, he didn't realize it would end our engagement. Actually he favored our marriage."

Thor said a nasty word and she blushed. "The only thing Milano favors is getting you."

"That's not true," she protested. "He thought your marrying me would be very practical. He still does. I wasn't interested in a marriage based on practical reasons before."

"Now you are?"

"I'm marrying you, aren't I?" She stared at him resentfully. "You act like you're the injured party. I'm the one who lived in a fool's paradise. I thought you loved me. Instead I learned the only reason you proposed was to keep Nick sweet during the negotiations. Can you deny it?"

His expression closed over. "I do deny it. I denied it last year and I deny it today. Do you honestly think I needed you to work the best deal with Nick and the Milanos? I didn't. But having me for a son-in-law would have been quite advantageous for Nick. He tried to make our marriage a stipulation, not me."

She jumped to her feet. "That's a lie! Don't you dare blame this on my father. He would never have done such a thing to me."

"And I would?"

"You proposed, didn't you? You tried to get the Milanos to break their contract with Constantine's and deal directly with you. When that didn't work, I was the next best choice. Get engaged to Nick's daughter and he'll give you the deal of a lifetime."

A muscle worked in his jaw. "You have it all figured out, don't you?"

"Yes." She lifted her chin, refusing to back down. "The truth is, you wouldn't be marrying me now if it wasn't for the Milano account. Deny that one if you can."

"I can't deny it," he bit out. "But I certainly regret it."

That hurt. Tears stung her eyes and she blinked hard to suppress them. "Marrying me last year was a smart business move, so you proposed," she said, her voice husky with emotion. "I was a means to an end for a man whose life is dedicated to the pursuit of business."

He came around the side of the desk and reached for her. Ignoring her resistance, he cupped her face. "So much passion. So much hurt. We did that to you, your father and I."

She shook her head. "Not Nick. Just you."

"Have it your way." He ran a gentle thumb across her eyelids, brushing away the tears that glittered on the tips of her lashes. "You're right about one thing. Business used to be the most important part of my life. For a good reason, or so I thought at the time."

"You haven't changed," she insisted, skittish in his embrace. "The only reason you're marrying me is that your deal with the Milanos is threatened and you'll do anything to save it."

"A rather extreme solution, don't you think?"

"One you were willing to choose before," she shot back.

"Perhaps." He ran his hands along her shoulders. "And what about you?" His fingers grazed the side of her neck, tangling in her hair. Her breath caught in her throat.

"I don't have a choice," she gasped. "You won't help me unless I marry you."

His hands tightened. "Meaning your business comes first, is that it?"

Meaning her *father's* business came first. There was a slight difference, though she didn't expect him to understand. If she'd been the only person affected, she'd tell him, her creditors, suppliers and brokers to all take a flying leap. But Constantine's future depended on her making the right choices.

She tried to pull away and met resistance. "Yes," she retorted rashly. "Constantine's comes first, as Thorsen's comes first with you."

"Your eyes betray you every time," he murmured. "Despite Nick and the Milanos and the contract, you wanted me. Only your pride got in the way."

"You certainly managed to strip that from me, didn't you?" she replied, smarting.

He laughed in genuine amusement. "It was a nasty job, but somebody had to do it." Then he lowered his head and kissed her. Thoroughly.

She should fight him, she kept telling herself. Her arms crept up his chest. She should protest. Her fingers sank into his thick tawny hair. At the very least, she shouldn't *enjoy* it. That was her final thought before she shifted closer, losing herself in his embrace.

Eventually he ended the kiss. "My parents are worried about your being all alone tomorrow night. They'd appreciate it if you'd come and stay with them."

Her automatic protest died on her lips. It was a sweet offer and one she'd be happy to accept. The idea of being by herself on the eve of her wedding didn't appeal in the slightest. She nodded. "Thank you. Tell them I'd like to very much. By the way," she thought to mention, "Sonja and Jordan filled me in about our wedding."

He smiled, his eyes gleaming a warm blue. "Oh?"

"Yes. Oh." She studied him curiously. "Do you know how hard it's been finding time for riding lessons? What gives? Why are we having such a fancy ceremony?"

He shrugged. "I explained that already. I intend to impress your suppliers and competitors. Believe me, this will do it."

"Still—"

He put a finger to her lips. "They won't buy a quick hole-in-the-wall affair, sweetheart. The more elaborate, the more convincing it will be."

She looked doubtful. "But all that trouble, not to mention the expense."

"My problem, not yours. I told you I'd take care of the details. And I will. You do your bit."

She smiled. "You mean, show up?"

"I mean, show up. I'll see you tomorrow at the rehearsal dinner. Until then, try and behave."

"Behave, as in stay away from Joe?"

He grinned. "It's a start." He dropped another kiss on her parted lips. "Andrea Thorsen. I like the sound of that."

She raised a hand to her mouth. The frightening part was she liked the sound of it, too.

CHAPTER FIVE

ANDREA STOOD by the window of her temporary bedroom watching the first hint of dawn lighten the August sky. Deep indigo and purple streaks tinted the calm waters of Puget Sound and crept toward the upper peaks of the Olympic Mountains. Her wedding day promised to be fair and clear, which considering Seattle's unpredictable weather patterns, came as some relief.

A light tap sounded at the door, and Jordan poked her head into the bedroom. "I thought I heard you stirring in here," she whispered, nudging open the door. Silverware rattled on the covered tray she carried. "Couldn't sleep?"

Andrea hurried over and took the tray, placing it on a small trivet table by the window. "Not a wink. If this is coffee, I'll be your best friend for life."

"Big deal. I already *am* your best friend for life." Seeing Andrea's disappointed expression, Jordan relented. "Yes, it's coffee and something to eat, as well."

"In that case, you can be my best friend in our next life, too." Andrea's stomach grumbled, reminding her that she'd only picked at last night's rehearsal dinner. Beneath the curious gaze of all Thor's relatives, her appetite had fast disappeared. "What have you brought me?"

Jordan chuckled, whipping off the linen napkin covering the tray. "Croissants with jam, my greedy chum. They're fresh from the oven. I gather Sonja couldn't sleep, either. I found her busy in the kitchen."

Andrea glanced nervously at the door and fiddled with the belt of her robe. "She decided not to join our little breakfast party?"

"She thought you'd prefer some privacy after last night's banquet." Jordan gave a reassuring smile. "You'll find Sonja's a very diplomatic mother-in-law."

Andrea nodded, knowing it was true. "You're right. She *is* diplomatic. She certainly coped well with all the, er, discussions, last night."

"Arguments, my dear. Don't bother being polite. They were gate-crashing, wall-tumbling, ear-blistering battles royal." Jordan took a large bite of her croissant. "Wasn't it great?"

"No."

The brunette made a face. "Look at how much we missed by growing up in small families. Besides, it isn't like the Thorsens were seriously angry or anything. They just love to squabble. It took me six whole months to figure that out. You're lucky enough to get the inside track from day one."

"Thanks so much," Andrea said dryly. "It's a wonder the banquet hall didn't demand a security deposit, considering the fuss Thor and Rainer made. I guess next time those two nearly come to blows I can say, 'Boys will be boys,' and send them to bed with no supper."

"You do that," Jordan replied, her eyes sparkling with secret laughter. "I'm sure Thor will thank you personally."

Andrea ignored the double entendre and sank into a chair. "I can't believe the size of his family," she commented, taking a reviving sip of coffee. "How many are there? I lost count at around fifty."

"There's eighty-three and—" Jordan patted her stomach, grinning "—two-thirds at last count. It changes on a daily basis, you know."

"I believe it." She picked up a croissant and broke off a flaky portion. "They all seem so happy for us."

"They are." Jordan studied her friend, her expression softening. "What's wrong, Andrea?"

She sighed. "I feel like such a fraud. What will they think when Thor and I divorce? They've gone to so much trouble and expense." She ticked off on her fingers. "There's the rehearsal dinner last night, the special costumes, carts and horses for the procession—"

"Not to mention the day and a half of celebrating after you're married."

"That makes me feel much better. Thanks!"

"You know I didn't mean it like that." Jordan hesitated, choosing her words with care. "Whose idea was it to have such an elaborate wedding?"

"Thor's."

"Why, do you suppose?"

"He explained that to me. It's to get the news out to my suppliers, so they'd think twice about giving me a hard time. With the Thorsens behind me—"

"Get real," Jordan broke in impatiently. "Formal announcements and a few follow-up phone calls would have been just as effective, don't you think?"

"I guess. But he said they wouldn't believe a small quick ceremony."

"And you bought that excuse?"

"I shouldn't have?"

"Sounds pretty lame to me."

Andrea frowned. She'd wondered about that, too, which only added to her unease. If such an elaborate setup weren't for her suppliers' benefit, why do it? "Then why do it?"

Jordan shrugged carelessly, taking another big bite of pastry. "Beats me," she mumbled. "Ask your husband."

"Husband-to-be."

"Picky, picky. A few more hours will take care of that. I'll tell you one thing." A sly look entered her gray-blue eyes. "You're the only one who thinks this marriage is temporary."

Andrea shot to her feet, nearly overturning her coffee cup. "Then you're all kidding yourselves," she insisted. "If it weren't for the problems at Constantine's, I wouldn't be marrying Thor."

"You sure?"

"Positive."

"You don't love him?"

"No."

"And he doesn't love you?"

"Absolutely not."

Jordan brushed the crumbs from the shelf of her stomach. "Sounds like an excellent foundation for marriage to me. Why don't I draw your bath? I think you should soak your head for a while."

Andrea's lips twitched. Jordan glanced at her and started to chuckle. The next minute they were both laughing helplessly. "You always were a brat," Andrea said, hugging her pregnant friend. "I'm glad you're going to be my sister-in-law. You're good for me, you know that?"

"I do. And it's about time you realized it, too." With that, Jordan trotted off toward the bathroom. She turned the tap on full blast and upended a jar of rose-scented bubble bath into the tub. "I'll also make you a little bet."

Andrea regarded her with suspicion. "What?"

"I'll bet by the time this baby makes its appearance in another two months or so, you'll have forgotten all about this temporary-marriage stuff. I win, you deliver a pallet-load of your biggest, juiciest ruby-red grapefruit to my produce market. Gratis, of course."

"Of course. And if I ... win." Andrea gulped. Why had she almost said "lose"?

"I'll give you a good swift kick and hope it implants a little common sense."

"What?"

"I mean, I'll find you two new customers."

Two new customers. She couldn't afford to pass that up. "You're on."

Jordan grinned. "I can taste that grapefruit already. Your bath, madam, awaits your pleasure." With a surprisingly graceful curtsy, she slipped from the room.

Andrea climbed into the steaming water, sliding down into the bubbles. Jordan was a good friend, if not terribly realistic. As yummy as pie in the sky might seem, it didn't have much taste.

She scooped up a mound of pink foam and blew gently into her cupped hands. A clump of bubbles spun into the air, floating high above. Thor didn't love her. He wanted her—she didn't doubt that for a minute. But it wasn't love.

She blew into her hands again. This time the pink foam burst into a thousand independent bubbles, raining down all around her. Regardless of what he'd said, business was his life, just as it had been her father's. To even imagine there might be another explanation asked for trouble of the worst kind.

She knew Thor well. If his account with the Milanos wasn't in jeopardy, he wouldn't be marrying her. Business first, pleasure second. That was Thor. A last puff of air scattered the remaining bubbles, leaving her hands empty. As empty as her marriage would be?

She sank deeper into the warm water and closed her eyes, her imagination defying all attempts to control. Images flashed through her mind. Jordan with a baby snuggled in her arms, perched atop a stack of grapefruit boxes, a smug expression on her face. Thor looking at her the way Rainer looked at his wife. Celebrating a fifth and a tenth and a fiftieth anniversary...

Close to her ear, the bubbles filling the tub began to burst, as temporary and ethereal as her daydreams. *Face facts,* she ordered fiercely. *It's not going to happen.* But that didn't prevent a wistful tear from escaping beneath one eyelid.

It crept slowly down her cheek, plopped into the soft pink foam and dissolved.

BY TEN O'CLOCK, her bedroom overflowed with helpful relatives-to-be. Each commented about her hair and makeup, her dress and jewelry. Finally, with a few pointed Norwegian words, Sonja cleared the room.

"Don't mind them," she told Andrea. "They all adore Thor and wish to help his bride any way they can."

"It's all right," Andrea assured her. She ran a cautious hand down the apron of her *bunad* and peeked at herself in the mirror. She couldn't believe the change in her appearance.

Sonja had coaxed her short flaxen curls into a sophisticated plait, a style flattered by the embroidered bridal crown that sat back on her head and tied beneath her chin. She fingered the trim on the bright red vest, aware her cheeks were almost as rosy. Excitement—and more than a touch of fear—gleamed in her large brown eyes, their color darkened with emotion.

"How do I look?" she asked, shy for perhaps the first time in her life.

Sonja gave an encouraging smile. "Stunning. It is good you are tall and slender. A few little tucks and the dress fits perfectly." She gave the green skirt a final twitch. "Of course, Thor would think you beautiful no matter what you wore. But in this... He will be very pleased."

Andrea busied herself with touching up her lipstick. She wanted Thor to be pleased. She wanted him to look at her with hot desire in his electric blue eyes, wanted to see the heat of passion creep across his high cheekbones. She wanted to hear the husky rasp in his voice when he spoke to her and know that she'd moved him as no other woman could.

Her hand trembled as she set the lipstick down on the dresser. Face it. She wanted an impossible fantasy, and the knowledge frightened her. It shouldn't matter what he thought and felt. Her happiness shouldn't depend on that. So why did it?

"It's time to go," Jordan announced from the doorway. "Rainer says everyone's lined up for the processional. The police report that all the streets are cordoned off and ready for the parade."

This was it. Andrea took a deep breath and left the bedroom behind, the full petticoats and skirt dancing gracefully around her white-stockinged calves as she moved. Once outside, she followed Sonja to the front of the line of carts and horses and buggies.

The pageantry of the scene amazed her. Everywhere she looked silver jewelry glinted and bright costumes flashed, the noisy crowd a happy festive sight. Carts stood loaded with children, as well as those who couldn't walk or ride the distance. Horses, curried and braided, stood patiently waiting, their elaborate bridles and oiled leather saddles gleaming in the warm sunshine.

She grinned, realizing someone had even thought to arrange for official "scoopers" to follow the parade and clean up any natural equine occurrences. Marco called to her from the crowd, and she waved, spotting several of her other employees, as well. Thank goodness she knew someone in this mass of humanity!

Then she saw Thor.

He stood by a pair of buff-colored horses, his expression remote and serious, his eyes as clear and light as the Seattle sky. She studied his costume, impressed at how naturally he wore the forest-green knickers and red, silver-buttoned vest, his muscular legs encased in white stockings almost identical to her own. He'd left his black overcoat open, the fabric stretched tautly across his shoulders.

As though aware of her scrutiny, he glanced her way and froze. His gaze swept over her with singular intensity, an unidentifiable expression flitting across his face. She paused, not quite certain of her role, ridiculously self-conscious as a result.

As though sensing her insecurity, he crossed to her side, standing tall and firm before her. *"God morn, Kjæreste,"* he said, bowing low.

Kjæreste. She'd heard Alaric use that word. Sweetheart, Sonja had interpreted. *"God morn, mannen man,"* she replied, giving him a curtsy in turn.

His eyes darkened and he took another step forward. She stared at him, instantly lost in his gaze. "Husband. I like the sound of that," he murmured. "You're beautiful."

She blushed, unable to say another word. He offered his arm, and she slipped her hand into the crook of his elbow, walking with him to their position in line. When she reached her horse, she stroked the velvet nose, smiling wryly. Finally Thor looked at her with all the passion and desire she wanted, and she was too abashed to respond. What had gotten into her?

"The horses are lovely. What kind are they?" she asked with genuine curiosity, as well as a desperate need to say something . . . anything.

"They're Norwegian fjord horses, very rare in this country."

Her brows drew together. That sounded expensive. "Where'd you get them?"

"From a cousin with a farm near British Columbia."

She relaxed somewhat. "*Another* cousin?"

"Frightening, isn't it?" Thor conceded, stroking the docile animal. "He breeds these beauties and loaned us two for today's parade as his wedding gift." He introduced her to the youth holding her reins. "This is his son, Erik. He'll lead your horse."

Andrea nodded in relief. Riding sidesaddle, she'd discovered, was not an easy task. Ever since she'd heard the details of their wedding, she'd dreaded this part. She'd been haunted by the image of tipping over and tumbling to the pavement, her skirts around her ears. Perhaps Erik would prevent that from happening. Better still, perhaps Erik could ride and she could lead.

Before she had time to suggest it, Thor placed his hands around her waist and, in a single easy movement, swept her off the ground and onto the horse. He waited until she'd settled into a comfortable position, shooting her a wicked grin. Taking his time, he rearranged her skirt and petticoats.

"Now you look perfect," he said as if to excuse his protracted attention.

She shivered, the brush of his callused fingers along her calves and ankles heightening her awareness of him. "Please," she murmured, darting a swift look around. "People are watching."

"We won't always be in the middle of a crowd," he answered her in an undertone. "What will you say then?"

Yes! "No." *Maybe.*

"We'll see when the time comes, won't we?" With seeming reluctance he released her and vaulted into the saddle of his horse. The animal shook its head, tiny silver bells attached to the halter tinkling gaily in the still morning air. "We should start in a few minutes—there's a certain order to all this, a tradition."

As though they'd heard him, the people joining in the parade scurried to get into line, their laughter and boisterous comments drowned out by the unexpected strains of a violin.

Andrea turned and spotted a man standing in front of the procession tuning up his instrument. Minutes later he broke into a lively march and danced into the blocked-off street. With a slap of the reins, a large, keg-laden cart driven by Caesar Milano rattled after him.

"Why is Caesar first?" she wanted to know.

"He's the *Kjøkemeister,* the host or master of ceremonies. In Norway, he'd be an important figure in the town, a prominent landowner or a successful merchant."

She shot him a speaking glance. "Very diplomatic of you to pick Caesar."

"I thought so." Thor's grin was carefree. "Since the host is in charge of the food and Milano's is catering our reception, it seemed a logical choice. It's also the host's duty to see all the guests get to the ceremony sober. And considering some of my relatives, he'll have his hands full."

She burst out laughing. "So why the keg?"

"They can have all they'd like of that. It's full of apple cider."

"Fermented by any chance?"

Thor shook his head. "Not according to Caesar. Though I didn't quite trust that gleam in his eye." The cart bearing his parents creaked down the driveway behind Caesar, and he explained, "Normally both fathers would come next. But since that's not possible, my mother is riding with Dad, instead of behind us with your mother."

"That means we're next." She stated the obvious.

"Are you nervous?"

"A little." She reached up to check that her bonnet hadn't slipped, tucking away a wisp of hair.

"It's perfect," he assured her. "You're perfect. I want to thank you."

She glanced at him uncertainly. "Thank me for what?"

He gestured around them. "For going along with all this. It can't be easy for you."

She didn't deny it. "Or you."

"It was my choice."

True. Which reminded her of Jordan's earlier comments to that effect. She fixed him with a determined stare. "I've been meaning to ask, why *did* you decide on such a—"

"Hang on, love. It's our turn," he interrupted.

Andrea's eyes narrowed. She had the distinct impression he knew what she was about to ask. Knew, and preferred to duck the question. Sonja turned and waved, the ribbons of her bonnet rippling behind her. Deciding to drop the issue, Andrea waved back and was forced to grab the pommel as her horse danced forward. Instantly Thor's arm shot out, steadying her.

"Easy," he murmured, his hand lingering on the curve of her elbow long after the necessity passed.

Crowds of people lined the street, fascinated by the spectacle. At first Andrea felt self-conscious, aware of being the cynosure of all eyes. She kept her gaze fixed on the horse's white forelock, reluctant to look left or right.

"Relax," Thor urged. "They're all happy for you. Try to enjoy yourself, sweetheart. This will only happen once your entire life. Savor it."

Andrea peeked at the sidelines. A small girl jumped up and down and pointed at her. Never before had she seen such an enraptured expression on a child's face. It gave her an odd humble feeling. She smiled hesitantly and waved.

Thor was right. She should savor these moments. Then and there she determined to save up each little memory, preserving it—for a time when memories were all she had left.

"How long will the ride take?" she asked after a few minutes.

"About an hour. Once there, we'll file into the church in the same order as the procession."

"The fiddler, too?" She pictured herself dancing down the aisle behind him. "That's different."

"No." Thor's glance was indulgent. "He's not allowed to enter. He'll stay outside and play until all the guests have arrived."

She scowled, taking insult for the poor man. Dancing down the aisle would have been fun. And it would have taken her mind off the real reason for her presence at the church. "Why can't he come in?"

Thor nudged his horse nearer and adjusted the tilt of her crown, his fingers lingering on her cheek. The crowd reacted instantly, the laughter and applause causing warm color to flood her face. He must have noticed her embarrassment, because he flashed her a teasing grin.

"Devilry, my love. Fiddles and fiddlers are not for the pious. The church frowns on all the carousing and carrying on that they represent."

Just then four riders, two on each side, broke rank, and with loud shouts galloped out ahead of the procession, disappearing down the street. Instantly Thor moved closer, grabbing her horse's bridle. His cousin, still in the lead, kept a firm hand on the reins, speaking softly to the startled animal.

Andrea clutched at the pommel, feeling oddly defenseless. In business, she'd always been the one in control. She'd made the decisions, handled the problems. For the first time she was aware of her vulnerability, aware that the man beside her served as her protector. It was a most unsettling—yet not altogether unpleasant—sensation.

"What—"

"Foreriders." He held up a hand. "Don't blame me. This one's Rainer's bright idea. I'd never heard of it before."

"What are they doing?"

"They ride back and forth between the church and the procession three times, raising as much ruckus as possible."

Her dark eyes gleamed with laughter. "That sounds like something Rainer would dream up. I assume there's a good reason for it?"

Thor lifted an imperious eyebrow. "Of course. It's to guard you against attack by evil powers."

Evil powers? With a grin she made a production of peering around. "Thank you. It seems to have worked. I feel much better knowing I'm so well championed."

He looked at her, his expression dead serious. "I'd never let anything hurt you," he promised.

For a long minute, she couldn't look away. She knew he meant every word. She also knew that nothing could hurt her more than Thor himself. How could he protect her from that? Only she could guard her heart against such a risk. And right now her guard was practically nonexistent.

The hour passed in a blur of sights and sounds and laughter. The people gathered along the way waved, and the members of the procession waved back, calling to friends and family. Finally they approached a large gray stone church set in the middle of a stand of pines. The fiddler stood on the church steps playing a lighter, gentler tune.

Thor dismounted and approached her horse. Without a word he reached up, gripped her waist and pulled her to him. She rested her hands on his shoulders, the firm muscles bunching beneath her fingers. Their eyes met and locked.

Slowly he set her on the ground, holding her in a secure embrace. Murmuring something in Norwegian, he lowered his head and settled his mouth on hers. She shut her eyes and clung to him, distantly aware of the cheering crowd, acutely aware of the incredible power of his kiss.

Eventually he released her. ''It's time,'' he said quietly, and took her hand, leading her up the steps of the church. In front of them walked Thor's parents, behind came their attendants, Rainer and Jordan. An organ played within, the lovely strains of Mendelssohn's *Midsummer Night's Dream* filling the chancel.

They paused in the vestibule, and Andrea's grip tightened in his. He leaned toward her, speaking close to her ear. ''It's all right, sweetheart. Don't panic. Look around. The greenery along the aisle is myrtle, symbolic in Norwegian ceremonies of Aphrodite. The candles are scented with spices. Can you smell them?''

She nodded, then glanced at all the decorations. ''And they've put white roses all around,'' she whispered. ''I've never seen so many.''

''Jordan told me they were your favorite.''

She knew his words were significant, but couldn't seem to think straight, nor did they have time for further conversation. The organ began to play the bridal march and they started down the aisle. At the altar they sat in the chairs provided. Once the rest of the congregation joined them, the ceremony began, taking on a dreamlike quality.

She knew the pastor spoke of marital responsibilities, but all she could think of was how irrevocably her life would change. He talked of faith and endurance, and she thought of her prisms and their promise of a better tomorrow. He mentioned love and commitment, something she knew couldn't be hers. Yet glancing occasionally at Thor, she felt strangely reassured. Instead of adding to her nervousness, his presence eased her fears.

Time passed. She watched the sun gleam through the stained-glass window, the muted colors enclosing them in a special world all their own. She listened to one of Thor's aunts sing, her lilting voice filling Andrea with hope and a quiet contentment. Thor's hand cupped her elbow. Together they stood and faced the solemn pastor.

He first addressed Thor. *"Å elske å ære hverandre inntil døden skiller dere ad?"*

"Ja," Thor spoke in a firm, carrying voice.

The pastor turned to her and repeated the question. Quietly Thor translated. "Do you promise to love and honor each other until death do you part?"

She hesitated, suddenly aware that she did want to make such a vow. She wanted to with all her heart. Tears pricked her eyes. It didn't matter what happened in the coming months. For today, and perhaps for tomorrow, she'd have Thor. She felt him beside her, and she realized that he and the entire congregation awaited her response. Did he doubt her answer? She smiled mistily, intense joy rising within her.

"I do," she said clearly.

Together they knelt for the blessing. It was almost over. In another minute, she'd be married to Thor. Standing once again, they exchanged rings. She stared at the gold braided band in wonder, noting how the intricate design had been crafted with such care and attention. Had he picked the ring specially for her? She glanced at him uncertainly, wishing she could ask.

"Join hands," the minister requested, interrupting her musings. In a booming voice he pronounced his final words: "I declare you to be husband and wife, to live together in good days and bad for the rest of your time on this earth."

They turned, facing the congregation. She heard the organ music swell and, hand in hand with Thor, started down the aisle. At the doorway of the church, the sound of cameras whirring and clicking startled her. With a muttered exclamation, Thor swept her into his arms and kissed her.

"Andrea Thorsen," he growled in a satisfied voice. "At last."

CHAPTER SIX

THE RIDE BACK to the Thorsens' seemed much shorter than the one to the church. She must be in a state of shock, Andrea decided. That would explain how she'd found the nerve to go through with the ceremony. But she had, and the proof weighed heavily on her finger. She twisted the braided gold band. It felt so...so permanent. *If only it was,* the contrary thought teased her.

"Andrea?" Thor caught her attention. "Are you all right?"

She fixed a smile on her face and waved to the crowd. "Of course. I'm fine."

"This part's almost over."

Was that regret she heard? She dismissed the thought. No. It must be relief. "We still have the reception to go," she reminded him. "Will it be at your parents' house?"

"Not a chance. Not with so many people. We've rented a banquet room at a hotel for later this afternoon." He glanced at her, his expression concerned. "You know we'll be expected to stay late?"

"Late?" She forced out a laugh. "Your mother told me traditional Norwegian weddings last for three days. We still have another twenty-four hours to go."

"We'll leave the party before then."

And go where? she wondered anxiously. She'd made her intentions clear about their living arrangements; they'd be separate. Could he be hoping for a traditional wedding night to match their traditional wedding? She set her mouth in a stubborn line. Well, hope was all he'd get. Right?

Unable to resist, she glanced once more at her wedding ring, shame rising within her. A business arrangement. She'd married to save her father's business. So noble. So self-sacrificing. So dishonest to the intent of the ceremony. *Face facts,* she ordered fiercely. She'd learned from the cradle that business came first. Always. She couldn't change that now.

Yet, close on the heels of truth came a wish. All she wanted, all she'd ever wanted, was to be loved for herself....

"We're here," Thor's voice interrupted her dreams. Once again he stood by her horse, holding out his arms. And once again, like a bird flying home to nest, she slipped into them. She trembled at his touch and knew he felt it.

"The wind's picking up," she said, attempting to excuse her shiver, not quite able to meet his eyes.

"It's all right to be nervous," he murmured.

She stepped away, annoyed. Was she so transparent? She didn't like her innermost feelings to be so apparent. Nor did she care to have him mention them aloud. Couldn't he, for once, turn a blind eye? At the very least, he could pretend to be a bit myopic.

"I'm not nervous," she attempted to lie. Unsuccessfully. She grimaced. There she went, flinging fibs when telling the truth wouldn't hurt anything more than her pride. Well, honesty came to those who exercised it. Maybe she should start warming up. "Okay. I'm nervous. Is that a crime?"

His lips twitched. "Not as far as I'm aware."

Retreating with dignity not quite intact, she managed a smile. "So what's next?"

"The photographer will take more pictures, but as soon as that's over, we can slip away and relax for an hour or so. Are you hungry? I can rustle up a few sandwiches and some of Caesar's apple cider." He grinned. "With any luck it'll be fermented, after all."

Her smile came more naturally this time. "Sounds good."

And it did. The thought of sneaking off and indulging in an impromptu picnic helped keep her sanity intact throughout the tedious photo session. The photographer seemed intent on snapping the "happy" couple from every angle, with every expression and in every setting, indoors and out. After two hours, Thor called a halt.

"You can take more at the reception," he instructed firmly. Grabbing Andrea by the hand, they raced for the house.

Thor ransacked the kitchen and loaded up a tray, deftly evading the well-wishers who crossed their path. "Show me which bedroom Mom gave you," he whispered in her ear. Moments later they'd slipped inside with no one the wiser, and closed and locked the door, the outside world held safely at bay.

Only then did Andrea feel the first hint of unease. She was holed up in a bedroom, all alone with Thor, or more precisely, with her *husband*. Not the smartest course to choose, if she hoped to maintain a prudent distance. She crossed to the window and untied the ribbons beneath her chin. Pulling off her crown, she set it carefully on a chair.

He placed the tray on the trivet table and stood behind her. Reaching up, he caressed the riot of curls tumbling free of her plait. "You're tense. Why?"

Honesty, she reminded herself, was still a virtue she held dear. Less now than earlier, true, but she'd managed it before and could again. "I'm uncomfortable being here. Alone. With you," she admitted baldly.

"Afraid I'll take advantage?"

"Yes."

"Smart girl."

She turned around to confront him, instantly wishing she hadn't. Unchecked passion marked his face. He stood close, his broad shoulders dwarfing her, his eyes ablaze with desire. He touched a curl at her temple, twisting it around his finger.

"Don't," she whispered.

He gave a husky laugh. "I have no choice." His hand moved over her cheek, sliding along her jaw to cup her head. He urged her the single step it took to bring them together. His hips and thighs pressed hard against her legs, the layers of petticoats creating a delicious friction.

The trembling started once more, shivering along her spine, filling her with nervous excitement. She put her hands up to stop him and instead found herself clutching his shoulders. He'd removed his overcoat and the rough linen of his red vest grated on her palms.

"Just a kiss, *kona mi,*" he muttered in her ear. "Just one."

My wife. Andrea stared at him, her brown eyes wide and apprehensive. She was his wife, and as such should be able to handle a single kiss. After all, it wasn't their first. So, why not? She lifted her lips to his, losing herself in the light tender contact. Instantly the kiss deepened, his mouth hard and insistent. On its heels came her reaction, eager and impassioned.

His hand wrapped around her, anchoring her to him. He'd kissed her often during last year's engagement, but she'd never felt this hot unrelenting demand. It left her frustrated, unfulfilled, aware that she could have so much more if only their marriage was real. Her hand slid upward, easing into his hair, and her fingertips brushed the small hammer earring he wore. She froze. Thor's hammer. A symbol of strength and power, of the ruthlessness with which he strove to win.

The reminder hit hard—their marriage and the true reasons behind it. She struggled for control. How could she feel like this, need like this, when they'd based their relationship on business? She groaned softly. Constantine's. That was why they'd married. Love—no, lust—had no place in her life.

"We can't," she murmured. "Please, stop."

He made a sound deep in his throat, his lips drifting from her neck to her shoulder. "You're right. This isn't the place and it definitely isn't the time."

Nor would it ever be, she determined. He swept away her defenses so effortlessly. A simple kiss, and she couldn't think straight anymore. Next time he touched her, she might not get a reprieve. Once he'd turned Constantine's around, he'd be out of her life, and where would she be? Shattered and alone, that's where. The same as last time.

She took a step back, and then another and another, with Thor's shrewd blue eyes watching her every inch of the way.

"Hungry?" he asked mildly.

"Starving," she admitted, striving for normalcy, as well as distance. "What did you bring?"

He walked to the table and uncovered the tray. "Chicken sandwiches and this." He held a bottle of champagne aloft. A teasing smile touched his mouth. "Beats apple cider, don't you think?"

It took a few quick twists for him to remove the wire and foil seal. With a muffled pop and a loud hiss, he uncorked the stopper from the bottle and filled two glasses. He crossed the room and handed her the fizzing wine.

"To you, my wife," he said, raising his glass. "May your marriage be everything you could wish."

She looked up at him uncertainly. She could wish for quite a lot, like a real marriage . . . like a real husband. But wishes like those were guaranteed to bring heartbreak. "To a successful—'' she couldn't quite bring herself to say *business* ''—venture.''

''Now to arrange our picnic.'' He opened a closet door and pulled out a quilt, which he spread on the plush rug. ''Bring the tray over, will you? Go ahead and kick off your shoes and relax. We have an hour or so before things get started.''

The time passed with surprising ease. If she didn't quite forget the passionate embrace they'd shared, she succeeded in putting it aside. They concentrated on their meal, the conversation light and amusing.

''Try this,'' he offered at one point, holding out a cracker dipped in salmon pâté. Before she could take it, he'd slipped the morsel between her lips, his thumb stroking the fullness of her mouth. ''Like it?''

The delicate flavor of the salmon eluded her, while his tender touch was etched in her memory. ''I love it,'' she admitted, not referring to the food.

He leaned closer and her heartbeat quickened. ''There's more. Do you want some?''

She licked her lips. ''Yes, please,'' she whispered, her eyes captured by the intensity in his. His head dipped lower, his breath warm on her face. Before he could act on the promise in his gaze, the handle of the door rattled.

''You guys in there?'' It was Rainer's voice, followed by a loud knock.

Andrea jerked away and Thor swore. He leapt to his feet and unlocked the door, yanking it open. ''What?'' he snapped, anger and impatience infusing the single word with a sharp warning.

Rainer grinned cockily. ''Naughty, naughty.'' He stuck his foot into the room, catching the door before it slammed shut. ''You'll have to come out of hiding now. The reception can't start until you're there. I volunteered to lead the search party."

"Thanks a lot."

"You're welcome." He stepped over the threshold, eyeing their picnic with interest. "Why don't you rejoin the family? I'll clean this up." He winked at Andrea. "That way I can give Jordan all the gory details."

Their return downstairs went almost unnoticed. Sonja alone stood vigil by the steps. "You're late," she scolded, her indulgent smile taking the bite from her words. "The limousine's ready to drive you to the hotel. I'll follow in a few minutes."

The reception passed in a blur of food and music and laughter. Rainer looked after the clients who'd attended, making sure they ate heartily of Milanos' fare. He gave particular attention to a sour-faced older man, keeping his plate well filled with cannoli, Joe's special dessert pastry.

"Who's that?" Andrea asked Thor, wondering why Rainer would waste his time with such an unpleasant-looking individual.

"Captain Alexander. He can swing a tugboat account in our direction, should he be so inclined."

Andrea smiled wryly. Of course. Business. She should have guessed. "I assume he isn't so inclined?"

"No, he isn't." Thor shrugged. "It's Rainer's problem. I'm off duty tonight. Come on. Let's enjoy."

They wandered through the room, smiling and laughing with friends and family. Food filled table after table, and beer, champagne or fruit punch filled every glass. Following dinner, the formal speeches began—funny, romantic, joyous and nostalgic. It seemed everyone had something to say.

Next came the cake cutting. Andrea stared in amazement at the huge multitiered cake Caesar wheeled out. Pure white roses and delicate pink buds covered the uppermost layer and cascaded artfully down the sides of the cake to form a wreath at the bottom. Speechless, she hugged Caesar, tears glittering in her eyes.

"I don't want to cut it," she whispered in his ear. "I'm afraid I'll ruin such perfection."

"What? Not taste Joe's masterpiece? You would insult him."

Thor showed no such hesitation. He cut them both a slice and, with a teasing glint in his eye, held the thickly frosted cake for her to try. "Come, my love. Have a taste," he murmured in her ear.

She nibbled warily at the cake, then laughed up at him, only to have her laughter melt away as he swept her into his arms and kissed the frosting from her lips.

Finally came the dancing.

Of all the cherished memories from that night, the part Andrea remembered most was the bride's waltz, or *brudevalsen,* as Alaric described it. The focus of every eye, she walked hand in hand with Thor to the empty dance floor. She envied the ease with which he turned her into his arms, his hand firm at her waist.

"Shall we?" he murmured.

"Yes. Please," she replied with heartfelt sincerity.

Andrea placed her hand on his shoulder, acutely aware of the contrast between the smooth silk of his shirt and the muscled power of his biceps. Before she had time to react, he pulled her close, holding her as though she was his most valued treasure.

She remembered every moment of that dance. She remembered his eyes; they were dark, serious and possessive. She remembered drifting across the floor; their steps matched perfectly. But most of all she remembered the kiss that ended their waltz; it was sweetly gentle, warmly passionate and as necessary to her as the very breath she drew.

Everything stayed clear in her mind, because it was that moment, lost in an impossible dream, when she realized she loved him still. She almost admitted it aloud. All that saved her was Rainer's interruption.

"There's trouble at Constantine's," he said in a low voice. "A break-in."

"Oh, no!" Andrea moved further into Thor's embrace. "Is anyone hurt? Willie, our security guard?"

"I don't think so. Marco's there with the police. They'd like one of you to come down and check on things."

Thor nodded, edging them discreetly from the dance floor. "I'll leave right now."

"I've arranged for a car to drive you to the house," Rainer continued, walking with them across the room. "You'll want to change before leaving."

"Thanks." Thor paused, glancing at Andrea. "Sweetheart, why don't you stay here with my parents? This shouldn't take long. I can get everything settled and return before I'm even missed."

She shook her head, adamant. "No way. It's my business and I'm coming."

He didn't bother arguing. "Rainer, make our excuses. With any luck, they'll think we've turned in for the evening."

"Right, but call me, okay? Things will continue here at least until dawn before the party moves to Mom and Dad's."

Without further discussion, they hurried to the car. In no time, they'd returned to the Thorsens', changed and were driving south through Seattle's dark deserted streets. Andrea stared fixedly out the window. How ironic to have their wedding day interrupted by business. Poetic justice, considering they'd married for that very reason.

She looked at Thor, saddened by his cool remote expression. He was no longer the man who'd held her so lovingly, who'd encouraged her to pretend, if only for the length of a dance, that their marriage could be real. Business first, she reminded herself. Business first.

They arrived ten minutes later. Police cars, lights still flashing, were parked outside Constantine's loading bay. Andrea jumped from the car. Not waiting for Thor, she ran for the steps. He caught her arm before she reached the dock.

"You stay with me or you stay in the car," he ordered through gritted teeth. "Your choice."

"This is my business," she maintained in a low voice. "Which means *my* responsibility."

"I don't give a double damn about your responsibilities. Now that we're married, your safety is *my* chief concern. I won't have you taking unnecessary risks. What's the decision, wife? Me or the car?"

He had a point. Running around half-cocked wouldn't accomplish anything. Nor would ticking him off. "Okay. I'll stay with you."

"Good choice," he muttered.

Then Marco came hurrying over. "It's all right," he claimed, relief lessening the lines that marked his aging face. "Nothing to get worked up about. Turned out to be a bit of vandalism. Must have been a couple of kids."

Thor's eyes narrowed. "How do you know?"

"They broke in and upset a few boxes is all. Scattered some produce around. Willie heard noises and investigated. Didn't see them, though."

"He's not hurt?" Andrea asked anxiously.

Marco addressed her for the first time. "He's fine, Ms. Const—er, Thorsen. I'm really sorry to spoil your wedding night like this."

"You were right to call us," Thor assured him. "I'd like to see the damage." He glanced down at Andrea. "Would you rather wait here with Marco?"

She didn't say a word, letting the fire in her eyes speak for her. Banishing her to the car wasn't enough, now he had to try it with the loading dock? He could forget that idea.

"Fine. Come on," he said, not debating the issue, and together they entered the warehouse.

Inside, the police were taking Willie's statement. In short order, Andrea answered the necessary questions, Thor acting as a protective buffer. Satisfied, the officers instructed her to file a report if she discovered any further damage.

After the police left, Thor turned to Willie and Marco. "Okay. Let's see what they did. Should we get cleaning crews in?"

"I can handle it," Marco assured him.

Thor smiled. "Thanks. But not tonight. Okay?"

Andrea let him take charge, her earlier anger dying. If anything, she experienced a vague sense of relief. After expending so much excitement and nervous energy on her wedding, she had very little left over for this latest crisis. As though he sensed her sudden fatigue, Thor clamped an arm around her waist, keeping her close to his side.

Willie showed them into the "wet room," the huge cooler filled with iced crates of broccoli, corn and lettuce. Several of the boxes were knocked off their pallet boards, the contents spilling across the floor.

"Is this all?"

Marco stirred uneasily. "Not quite," he muttered. He shot a quick meaningful glance at Andrea. "Maybe you'd like to stay here with Willie while I take Mr. Thorsen."

She resisted the temptation to remain behind, certain Marco had an excellent reason for his reluctance to show her the rest. Her lips firmed. As owner of Constantine's she couldn't afford to give up that much control, especially since Thor's advent in her life was temporary. No, she corrected herself firmly, she wouldn't give up control even if it was permanent.

"I appreciate your concern, Marco, but I'd rather get it over with." She smiled. "I won't fold at the sight of a little waste and ruin, I promise."

He nodded unhappily. "Upstairs."

She knew what to expect even before he opened the door to her office. Still, a shock of fury rushed through her at the sight of corn and melting ice dumped over every inch of the room. She turned away, exhaustion following swift on the heels of her anger, and stepped directly into Thor's arms. This wasn't a couple of schoolboys bent on malicious mischief. This was deliberate. And aimed at her.

So much for not folding.

"Come on," Thor said, his voice ragged with suppressed emotion, his arms tight around her. "We're out of here. Marco, could you arrange to have this cleaned up by Monday?"

"Sure thing, Mr. Thorsen."

Thor led her down the steps and onto the loading dock. She took deep gulps of air, tears beginning to choke her. Without a word, he swept all sixty-eight inches of her into his arms and carried her to the car.

"Don't, sweetheart," he muttered close to her ear. "They're not worth it." He tucked her into the passenger seat and then climbed in behind the steering wheel.

"How could anyone do such a despicable thing?" she demanded through her tears. "And why? Revenge?"

A muscle moved in his jaw. "I don't know. But I swear to you, I'll find out. Don't worry. I'll take care of everything." He started up the car and threw it into reverse.

She stared at the night through unseeing eyes. Thor would take care of everything. That's what he'd promised and that's why she'd married him, right? She needed to rebuild Constantine's and earn a decent profit. She had obligations to meet and debts to pay off while keeping both the Thorsens and the Milanos happy. And the only way she could do all that was to marry Thor.

Now they'd hit the first little snag, a minor bump in the road. Thor's job required him to mend the snags and smooth out the bumps. She shouldn't mistake his concern for anything other than a businesslike expedience. Certainly she shouldn't mistake it for actual caring—or love.

So why did she have this urge to shunt the whole sorry situation off on the first willing party? Jack Maxwell would buy Constantine's. His offer might be just shy of an insult, but she'd been insulted before and lived to tell of it. Of course if she sold, Thorsen's would lose the Milano account, and she'd lose the Thorsens. More specifically, she'd lose Thor. Which put her on the losing end of the stick no matter which choice she made.

The car pulled to a stop, and Thor switched off the engine. Awakening to her surroundings, Andrea looked around. They weren't at his parents', nor at a hotel. In fact, she didn't recognize this place at all. "Where are we?" she asked suspiciously.

He got out, not answering. Walking to her side of the car, he opened the door. "Welcome home."

Welcome home? As in, *his* home? Turning her head, she stared through the front windshield, refusing to budge. She wouldn't go in. The temptation was too great and her resistance too low. "Forget it."

"You can't stay there all night," he said in mild tones.

"Sure I can."

"It's starting to rain."

"I like rain."

"I do, too. But I like it better from the inside looking out."

Her smile was smug. "I am inside."

His brows lowered. "Not for long."

He reached past her and unbuckled the seat belt. One strong jerk sent her tumbling from the car and into his waiting embrace.

"I can't stay here!" she wailed. "This is your place. Besides, we have an agreement."

His voice held patience. "You're in shock, sweetheart—the wedding, the reception, the break-in at Constantine's. You'll feel better once we're inside." He tugged gently at her hand. "Come on."

"No." She folded her arms across her chest and stared at him with mulish obstinacy. She would not go into *his* house. Not that she cared to go to the loft at Constantine's. She shivered. A hotel would do nicely. "A hotel will do nicely," she informed him.

He tried reason. "It's late. We have no luggage. We're tired and getting wet."

"Hotels are used to late, luggage-less, tired and wet patrons." She sniffed. "I'll bet it's their specialty."

A muscle leapt in his jaw. She doubted he'd try patience or reason again. Which, if the expression in his eyes was anything to go by, left murder. "Sometimes action accomplishes far more than words," he muttered. "And with you I believe that's a fact."

Obviously deciding on an alternative just shy of mayhem, he leaned down, thrust his shoulder against her hips and lifted. Clamping an arm around the back of her knees, he carried her—protesting all the way—into the sprawling ranch-style bungalow.

"We are now out of the rain, away from nosy neighbors and more comfortable," he said, dropping her to her feet. "You have my permission to argue all you like."

She took a deep breath. "My pleasure! You—"

"I'm going to shower, have a drink, make a few phone calls and go to bed." He turned and disappeared down the hallway.

She stared after him in disbelief. "A fine way to treat your wife on her wedding night!" she shouted without thought.

He reappeared, stripped of his shirt. "It would be my pleasure to treat you like a wife on her wedding night." He pointed to a door. "That's my bedroom. I'll be with you soon."

Mutely she shook her head. "Our agreement," she croaked.

He walked toward her and she squeezed her eyes shut, afraid to watch. Oh, Lord, she shouldn't have riled the man. Now he'd want to kiss her and touch her and do wild and wonderful things to her.

He cupped her chin, lifting her face. "Look at me, sweetheart," he ordered in a quiet voice.

Nervously she pried open an eyelid and peeked up at him. He didn't seem furious. He didn't even appear mildly upset. He appeared... Darn it all, he appeared downright sympathetic. "Yes?"

"There's nothing to fear. I haven't forgotten our agreement. Bringing you home seemed the best option. You shouldn't be alone, and I don't think it's appropriate to return to my parents'. If you'd rather, we could go to your place."

Her eyes widened. To the loft? He'd kill her for sure if he ever found out about that. "No, no. I don't think that's such a good idea."

"Fine. I have a spare bedroom. You can sleep there. As to my intentions, I'll say it again. I'd like to shower. I have to call Rainer and sort through a few problems. I could use a drink, preferably something strong. After that I'm going to bed and to sleep." His fingers lingered on her cheek for a second longer before his hand fell away. "That's it. I suggest you do the same."

So much for his being consumed with mindless passion. She felt her energy level ebb to a new low. "You're right," she murmured. "I'm sorry I overreacted."

"Forget it. It's been a long and trying day." She winced and he sighed, rubbing a hand over his hair-matted chest. "I didn't mean it like that. Why don't you shower first? I'll call Rainer. Okay?"

She nodded, furious with herself for being so sensitive, more furious, though, for not being able to drag her gaze from the hypnotic play of his hand on his chest. It must be sleep deprivation. She'd heard very strange stories about people who'd gone long periods of time without sleep. She considered. It must be well after one in the morning, and she'd been up since six. Did nineteen hours qualify? Reluctantly she decided not.

"Andrea?" Was that a hint of exasperation she heard?

"It's okay," she reassured him. "I'm not sleep deprived. I'll go have my shower now."

If he felt confused, he didn't show it. "Right," he agreed, his expression carefully serious. "I'll see you in the morning."

She took a deep breath and moved toward the bedroom he'd indicated. She opened the door and looked in. Nice. It was compact and attractive in bold blues and golds. The perfect room for her nonexistent wedding night. Blinking away tears, she crossed to the adjoining bathroom. She stripped off her jeans and shirt, and stepped beneath the hot spray.

It felt wonderful to wash away all the stress and strain of the past several hours. If only she could wash away her heartache, as well. But heartache, she'd learned, was inscribed with an indelible marker.

She dried herself with a big fluffy towel and glanced at her heap of discarded clothing. It would be nice to wear pajamas, or a nightshirt at least, but she hesitated to ask anything more of Thor. Dismissing the problem, she gathered up her clothes and carried them into the room.

To her delight a simple white shirt was spread across the bed. She dropped her clothes and held the fine silk to her body, her flushed skin showing through the translucent material. Unquestionably Thor's shirt. It was so large she couldn't mistake it for anyone else's. She slipped her arms into the sleeves and smiled. What a thoughtful gesture.

Engulfed by the excess material, she rolled up the cuffs. Not that the size really mattered, she decided, too exhausted to care, too exhausted to think straight. With a wide yawn she tumbled into the bed and dragged the covers up to her ears.

Her wedding day was officially over. Too bad business spoiled it. Her eyes shot open in sudden realization. Too bad *her* business spoiled it. She sat up, a frown creasing her brow. Here she'd accused Thor of putting business first, and all along it had been her fault and her business. How appalling. She burrowed beneath the blankets, unsettled and more than a little guilty. How very appalling.

ANDREA STIRRED and peered around the darkened room. She wasn't quite certain what had awakened her, a strange noise perhaps, but once awake, she found sleep elusive. She heard the noise again, identifying it this time as the muted clink of glasses. Throwing aside the covers, she padded from the room. Farther down the hallway, a lone light gleamed from an open doorway and she moved toward it.

"Thor?" she called, shading her eyes against the brightness.

"Couldn't sleep?" His tired voice came from the depths of the living-room couch. "I couldn't, either. Why don't you join me?" He shifted to one side, and after a momentary hesitation, she curled up next to him, using his shoulder for a pillow.

She glanced at the glass he held. "What are you drinking?"

"Orange juice. Like some?"

"Thanks." She took a healthy sip. "Why couldn't you sleep? Because of Constantine's—" she hesitated, wondering if she should be pursuing this conversation, coward that she was "—or because of our marriage?"

"Yes."

"Oh." That about covered it.

He took the glass from her hand and finished it off, setting it on the table behind them. At the same time, he snapped off the lamp, plunging the room into a comfortable darkness.

"I could have killed Hartsworth for trying to harm you," he commented in conversational tones.

She stirred uneasily. "You're sure he's behind it?"

"Aren't you?"

There wasn't any doubt in her mind. "Yes."

"So am I." She could feel his tension. "He won't do it again. I've seen to that."

She swallowed. "How?"

"It's probably best you don't know. Suffice to say I've sent a clear message to all comers. They'll keep their hands off you."

"You mean Constantine's."

He shrugged. "It's all the same."

"No. It's not. Constantine's is business, I'm—"

"My wife," he interrupted, his voice rising a notch. "I stood before a minister and promised to protect you today, and that's precisely what I intend to do."

"I remember the love and honor part." She frowned, struggling to recall all the minister had said. "When did that protect business come into it?"

There was a long moment of silence. "It was in Norwegian," he explained tightly. "Protect and, uh, take care of. Something like that."

A tiny smile tugged at her lips. "Right. You must have forgotten to translate that bit."

"Must have." He shifted, tucking her more firmly against his hip. "I've been thinking about our living arrangements. I want you to move in here."

What should she say to that? Something casual. Keep her answer nice and amusing—and safe. "Forget it."

He wasn't amused and she wasn't nice and safe. "I won't forget it! You stood before that minister and made a few vows, yourself."

"I never promised to—"

"Live with me. Yes. You did."

Yeah right. "Yeah, right. When?"

"Sometime after the beginning and before the end."

"That's an expedient answer, if I ever heard one. Let me guess. It was in Norwegian and another of those bits you neglected to translate."

"You got it. Love and honor, be protected and live with until death, et cetera, et cetera. That's how it went."

Of all the lying, conniving, rotten... "I can't."

"What do you mean, you can't?"

"You should have told me that before. You see, I already made a vow, which precludes your vow."

He stilled. "What the hell are you talking about?"

"A vow to my dead Aunt, er, Matilda. I promised never to live with a man in a temporary relationship. Ours is a temporary relationship. Therefore I can't live with you. Sorry, but a vow *is* a vow."

"You're making that up." He rolled over on top of her, crushing her into the cushions. "It's too dark. I can't see your eyes. But if I could, they'd tell me you're lying."

She didn't dare say a word, not with every inch of her in a stage-one red alert.

He exhaled gustily. "Okay. I give up, you can stay at your place. For now."

"Gee, thanks."

"Fair warning, though. Take all the rope you want and run as far as you can," he advised. "Because one day soon, you'll reach the end of your line. And then I'm going to haul you in, hog-tie you and cart you off home." With that threat, he wrapped his arms around her and reversed their positions.

"What are you doing?" she gasped in alarm.

"If tonight is all I'm to have, I think I'll enjoy it. Try and sleep, sweetheart, because you're stuck with me until morning."

Well, of all the nerve! After a moment's thought, she snuggled into his embrace, a secret smile on her lips. If she was stuck, why struggle? She wound her arms around his waist. She'd just have to suffer. Her smile widened. She could learn to enjoy martyrdom.

CHAPTER SEVEN

ANDREA AWOKE to the rhythmic sound of rain and to the soft muted gray of morning. She blinked sleepy eyes, her gaze roaming the living room. Against the far wall she noticed a glass case containing a huge Viking ship. It was a wooden model and exquisitely crafted. Had Thor built it? she wondered, impressed. She would have to give it a closer examination. But not just yet.

Warm and cozy, she resisted the urge to move. She was blissfully content and darned if she'd do anything to upset that. It would take something major, something along the lines of dynamite, to blast her from her current position.

The unyielding body supporting her should have felt hard and uncomfortable. But it didn't. It felt warm and accommodating. The muscular chest that pillowed her head should have given her a stiff neck. Instead it filled her ear with a steady, comforting heartbeat, lulling her toward slumber. The thick hairs resting beneath her palm should have prickled and itched. Admittedly they did tickle a little. But mostly they teased, creating a longing within her to caress the powerful chest they covered.

Her fingers quivered, and giving into an urgent longing, she burrowed delicately into the red-tinged hairs.

"I like you in my shirt," a drowsy voice rumbled beneath her cheek, stilling her roving hand dead in its tracks. "I picked it out specially, you know."

She gave a huge yawn, stretching as though she'd just awakened. "Thanks. You have my undying gratitude."

"Aren't you going to ask why I picked it out specially?"

"No." She shifted closer, hoping he'd go back to sleep so she could continue her surreptitious explorations. How often would this chance come along?

"I'll tell you, anyway. It's see-through," came the self-satisfied explanation.

She froze. "Say what?"

"Mmm-hmm." He wound his arm around her, tracing a line down her spine. "I can see the most delectable little mole square in the middle of your back. Right...there."

"Stop that!" She squirmed beneath his finger. "I'm ticklish."

"Tell me about it. Not that I'm complaining. Feel free to jump around like that anytime."

Understanding dawned an instant later and she went rigid in his arms. "I think I'll get up now."

He choked on a laugh, his finger drifting lower. "Did you also know that you have this tiny star-shaped scar right on the curve of your—"

With an outraged yelp, she leapt off him. Slapping her hand to a rounded cheek, she raced into the bedroom and slammed the door shut. She lifted his shirt and peered over her shoulder at her backside. Sure enough, there it was—a tiny star-shaped scar. The rat. She glared at the door. "Go ahead. Yuk it up. We'll see who laughs last, Mr. Hammer-ear."

The rest of Sunday passed quickly and pleasantly. As though by mutual consent, they kept it light, never once broaching the subject of Constantine's or the break-in. Knowing she loved him and aware of how short a time they'd have together, each moment became precious. She played with the idea of trying for a more permanent marital arrangement. But something stopped her, some inner protective fear.

Later that day, she asked him about the Viking model and learned that Thor had indeed built the longship by hand. Such care and attention, she realized in awe, so much patience and determination. It was a true reflection of the man.

As evening approached, he suggested she stay another night, and she didn't argue. She still couldn't face returning to Constantine's. She did, however, insist on picking up her own car. Monday meant work, and she didn't want to depend on Thor for everything.

Curled up in bed Sunday night, she reviewed the events of the past three days, surprised at how well their marriage seemed to work. The ceremony had gone without mishap. Thor's family was a delight. And they'd met their first "business" crisis head on. Or at least, Thor had. So far, she decided with satisfaction, so good.

THE NEXT TWO WEEKS passed with amazing speed. Andrea insisted on moving "home." To her surprise, and secret disappointment, Thor didn't protest. Because her nerves weren't quite up to living at Constantine's, she checked into a motel. That provided her with a temporary solution. Now with funds running short, she had only one option remaining—to return to the loft.

She grimaced, leaving the wet room and moving on to the fruit cooler. She didn't have further burglaries to fear, she argued with herself, checking her inventory sheet. Thor had taken care of that. Which meant she could sleep here again, starting tonight. So why did she dread the idea. She kicked a pallet board loaded down with d'Anjou pears. She dreaded it because she was still a little frightened.

Arms closed around her and she shrieked in panic.

"Ah, *cara,* I find you." Joe planted a smacking kiss on each of her cheeks and grinned. "I scare you good, huh? How you been? You look great. I like your wedding very much."

Her heart rate slowed from the speed of light to something approaching the speed of sound. "You certainly got into the spirit of things," she managed to joke.

"Yes, I ride very good on the horse." He leaned closer, whispering in her ear. "I blow kisses to many women and make them blush." He ran a finger over his mustache and waggled his dark brows in an exaggerated manner.

Her mouth curved upward. "I don't doubt it."

"Don't doubt what?" a voice interrupted them.

With a guilty start, she turned around. "This is getting to be a habit," she complained to her husband.

"A bad habit. Perhaps if you didn't have so many intimate conversations with Milano, it wouldn't happen as much."

Joe cleared his throat. "Why, Thorsen. Good to see you. I congratulate you on your marriage."

Thor folded his arms across his chest and stared down at the shorter man. "Are you here on business or just here?"

"I think if I am very smart, I should say business." Joe's dark eyes twinkled irrepressibly. "Business."

"Which is?"

"Ah, *cara.*" Pointedly Joe turned his back on Thor and snatched up Andrea's hands, refusing to relinquish them despite her insistent tugs. "The produce this week has been *magnifico.* I come to tell you how much I love your, er, grapefruits."

"That tears it!" Thor started for Milano.

Joe, with an agility born of long experience, danced sideways away from the enraged husband, still clinging to Andrea's hands. He spoke fast. "Your peaches, so pretty and sweet. Your apples, they are fat and crisp and juicy—a little tart, true—but I quite like the tarts.''

"Out! Before I make applesauce of your face."

Joe grinned mischievously. "And your vegetables, sheer heaven. Shall I tell you about the tiny flower of your broccoli?''

Thor grabbed Andrea around the waist. "You do and your nose will resemble tomato paste.''

Joe kissed Andrea's fingertips. "I tell you, anyway. I love them very much. Then there is the carrots, so long and firm and...and orange. And the baby radish—" he licked his lips "—they sting my tongue like a lover's bite. How about—"

"This is not a tug-of-war," Andrea objected, the pull on her hands and at her waist becoming a tad too strong. "And I am not a piece of rope.''

"Maybe not," Thor said in no uncertain terms. "But you're almost at the end of one. Be careful you don't hang yourself. In the meantime—" he forcefully disengaged her fingers from Joe's "—we're gone.''

"But I did not mention the cucumber," Joe protested.

"You keep your cucumbers away from my wife." With that, Thor hustled Andrea out of the cooler.

"You are not jealous, Thorsen?" Joe's laughing voice followed them. "I would not like you to be jealous of me.''

Andrea stopped dead in her tracks. Jealous? Thor? Could he be? Grinning like a fool, she ran to catch up with her husband. That possibility hadn't occurred to her before. But remembering his frequent clashes with Joe gave her food for thought and cause for hope.

"We'll talk in your office," he announced over his shoulder.

"I take it I don't have any choice?" she said, panting.

"No.''

Thor stepped into the room and turned to confront her. Without another word, he slammed the door closed behind them and snatched her into his arms. "I've changed my mind about a few things, starting with this."

He cupped her head in his two hands and kissed her, a hungry, angry kiss. She fought him for a full thirty seconds—she did have her pride—before gracefully giving in. The kiss went on and on, his mouth ravishing hers as though he'd missed her with as much desperation as she'd missed him. Clearly, fifteen days apart was fifteen days too long.

"The next time Milano so much as touches even your fingernail, I'm going to break his face," Thor muttered, his teeth nipping at the lobe of her ear.

"He doesn't mean anything by it." She stumbled to a halt as his tongue grazed her neck. "He...he's like that with everyone."

"Not with me, he isn't. And not with my wife."

"Temporary wife."

He pulled away, glaring down at her. Dark red color suffused his lean cheekbones, his eyes glittering with a dangerous blue light. "Did you tell him our marriage is temporary. Is that why he's here?"

"No—"

"He's not to know. Ever."

"He's bound to find out eventually."

"How?"

She sighed. "When we divorce."

A strange smile touched his mouth, and he bent down to kiss her again, gently, tenderly, with a sweet passion that left her clutching his shirt to remain upright. "So long as it's not before then, I'm satisfied." He gave an impatient groan. "My house is empty without you. When are you moving home?"

She stared up at him in confusion. "What are you talking about now?"

"I'm talking about changing the rules. I've missed you, and if that kiss is anything to go by, you've missed me. There's no reason we shouldn't enjoy our marriage, however long it lasts."

"Forget it." She stepped free of his arms, furious at him for assuming so much, but even more furious with herself. For a minute, she'd almost believed in the possibility of dreams becoming reality. "If that's the only reason you're here, you can leave. I have work to do."

He hesitated, clearly preferring to argue. Then he relented. "It's the most important reason I've come, but not the only one. If you insist, we'll discuss our other problem."

Uh-oh. That didn't sound good. "Other problem?"

"You got it. *This* other problem." He pulled an invoice from his pocket and handed it to her.

She glanced at the pink slip of paper and shrugged. "It's a bill."

"I know—it's *your* bill." A muscle jerked in his cheek. "Why is it still so high? As Milano mentioned, the quality has been fantastic."

She grinned. "Great."

"Not great," he contradicted. "The prices have been even more fantastic. Or perhaps I should say exorbitant."

Her grin faded. "Not great? I don't get it. I give you a standard markup over cost. How can I be so far out of line?"

He inspected her office. "I think I'm beginning to understand," he muttered.

"Understand what?"

He gestured at her stacks of paper. "Look at this place. It's total chaos. How can you run a business with all your records piled six feet high on every available surface?"

For the first time, she saw her room as he did. Thor had a point, she conceded. An outsider could easily get the wrong impression. "I know where everything is," she explained. "Tell me what you want and I'll get it."

He checked the bill. "Cauliflower. Let me see your bill of lading for cauliflower."

In three seconds flat she had it in his hand. "Well?" she asked with a superior smile.

He compared the two papers. "I'll admit you've given us a reasonable markup. So that's not the problem. How do you order your produce?"

"We have set farmers and brokers we deal with, depending on the time of year and where the item originates. When we're low, we call and order. Sometimes they call us with a special deal."

"And they tell you the price?"

"Yes."

"Do you dicker with them?"

She looked at him in bewilderment. "Dicker?"

"Bargain, haggle, negotiate, hack. You know, dicker. Everyone does it. That's how it works." He eyed her with suspicion. "I thought you'd been brought up in this business."

She flushed at his unwittingly discovering her major weakness. "I was."

What she hadn't been brought up to do was *run* Constantine's, mainly because her father hadn't bothered to teach her. He hadn't anticipated the need. Nor, she admitted honestly, had he wanted to give a woman that much control. Nick had always believed in keeping his hands firmly on the business reins, which included the buying and stocking of inventory. Could she help it if her specialty leaned toward PR and bookkeeping?

In the past seven months, she'd given it her all. Since her father's death she'd spent every waking moment playing a massive game of catch-up. Unfortunately every time she thought she had the game nailed, someone came along and changed the rules.

"Well?" he asked impatiently.

"I know what dicker means." She just didn't know how to do it.

"She knows what dicker means. Bring out the champagne and pop the corks." Thor closed his eyes, swearing beneath his breath. "Let me guess what the real problem is here. You're flying blind and too proud to admit it."

"That's not true, I—"

"I assumed, a big mistake I'll concede, that at the very least you were somewhat familiar with this business. More fool me."

"I am. I do—"

"I also assumed, another big mistake, that your problem was with greedy suppliers and competitors taking advantage of a woman."

"It is, but—"

"It never once occurred to me that you stunk at your job."

"I don't!" It took every ounce of determination to sit on her druthers and tell him the truth. "I'm inexperienced, not bad at my job."

"Inexperienced?" He shot the question at her. "Why?"

Boy, did it hurt to explain how little her father trusted her, or anyone, for that matter. "Nick always handled the purchasing end of things," she muttered reluctantly.

"That's not customary, is it?"

She shook her head. "Other wholesale houses let the salesmen take care of it. I have Marco supervising the inventory, but since purchases were Nick's job, I took that over."

"Regardless of whether you could handle it." It was a flat statement. "What else is there?"

She stirred uneasily. "What do you mean?"

"You're being evasive," he snapped. "The eyes, sweetheart, remember? They're a dead giveaway. What else have you neglected to confess? What other problems should I know about?"

The loan. She'd kept very, very quiet about that. It wasn't really a problem. True, she owed the money. But with the Thorsens' help, she'd have no trouble meeting her monthly obligation to the bank. Perhaps she should mention it. For her father's sake and for her own peace of mind, she would be a wee bit tactful how she phrased it.

"There are some minor outstanding bills," she admitted, stretching the truth more than a little. "As a result, Constantine's isn't as profitable as it used to be. But we can meet all our expenses if we're careful. With the Thorsens' backing, we should be able to rebuild to where we were a few years ago."

"What outstanding bills—"

The phone rang, and murmuring an insincere apology, Andrea answered it. "It's Rainer," she said, handing Thor the receiver.

"Yes, what's up?"

She studied him while he spoke, smiling despite herself. He'd run a distracted hand through his hair, ruffling the russet-tinged waves and giving him an impatient demanding edge, a side of him she'd experienced more than once. He answered his brother's questions with brisk efficiency, his shrewd intelligence fascinating to observe.

She'd always liked watching him, aware from the start of their mutual attraction. The very first minute he'd strode onto Constantine's loading dock, she'd felt an inexplicable tug of desire. He'd felt it, too. Even after she'd broken their engagement, she'd known he still wanted her. He'd just never allowed passion to overrule his common sense.

It was the same now. The moment something threatened his business he'd moved rapidly to counter it, willing to do whatever was necessary to correct the situation. If there'd been another easier solution to their current problem, his ring wouldn't be on her finger.

She balled her left hand into a fist and shoved it into the pocket of her jeans. What couldn't be changed could be ignored. Her gaze sought Thor. Well, if not ignored, at least held at a safe distance.

He hung up and glanced at her. "Where were we?"

Discussing her outstanding bills. Not that she intended to remind him of that. She'd changed her mind about confessing all. Thor wasn't the only one capable of putting business first. "You were analyzing my professional failings," she told him coolly. "You'd decided I was lousy at my job, and that, not unscrupulous businessmen, is responsible for Constantine's downfall."

"Ticked you off, did I?"

"Yes. Do you have any solutions to offer? Helpful solutions, that is?"

"For our business problems or our personal ones?"

She gritted her teeth. "Business. As far as I'm concerned that's all there is between us." She smiled tightly. "Nothing personal."

He lifted an eyebrow. "You seem to have suffered a slight memory lapse, sweetheart." He walked toward her with a rakish grin that would have done Joe proud. "But you're in luck. I know how to fix it."

"No!"

"I've been thinking," he continued, coming closer. "You've had a couple of weeks to get used to our marriage. It's time we set up some new ground rules."

"Forget it." She put some distance, and several five-foot stacks of paperwork, between them. "I like the current ground rules just fine, thanks."

"You move in with me."

"No way."

"Husbands and wives are supposed to live together."

"I made a vow, remember? To Aunt Martha."

"Matilda."

"Whomever."

He shrugged. "We won't tell her. I'll cook. You can clean."

"I hate to clean."

"You cook and I'll clean."

"I don't know how to cook."

"We'll hire a housekeeper." He knocked over three stacks of paper and caught her before she could scramble away. Sitting down in the chair behind her desk, he pulled her onto his lap. "I wouldn't wiggle like that, my love." He kissed the corner of her mouth. "It's very distracting."

She froze. "The business," she prompted desperately.

"Right. We'll work together while I help you get a handle on the purchases. You're not using Nick's office. If you don't have any objections, I'll operate from there."

"I'm objecting all over the place," she complained, "not that it's doing any good."

He continued as though he hadn't heard. "My secretary can help for a few weeks and clear up any backlog."

"That sounds expensive."

"Not at all. I pay my secretary. It won't cost you a dime."

She thought about it. She really did need help. If, between them, they could straighten out the remaining glitches in Constantine's operation, having to work with Thor on a daily basis would be a small price to pay. She rolled her eyes. Who was she kidding? Working with Thor every day would be the next best thing to nirvana, something she should avoid at all costs.

"Agreed," she finally said. "But I won't move in with you."

"You'd like to compromise. An excellent business ploy. You're a fast learner. Okay, I accept. You don't have to move in with me. I'll move in with you."

"No!" she exclaimed. "We can't. That's not what I meant."

He shook his head. "You know compromise doesn't work that way. I give in on something and you give in on something." His hand moved in small circles up her arm. "I'm giving in on *where*. Now it's your turn to give in."

She wanted to. Lord, did she want to. She wanted to give in, give up, give way and give over. Only a strong instinct for self-preservation saved her. In less than six months she'd have to live with today's decision. If she hoped to survive that time, she had to stand firm. Please let her stand firm!

"You can stop stroking my arm. It isn't going to work." It took every ounce of determination to keep her voice level. "I'm giving in on business. You're giving in on our living arrangement." She even managed a smile. "Or lack thereof."

His hand crept up to the nape of her neck. "Are you sure?" he asked with regret.

"Positive." Being very careful not to wiggle, she eased off his lap. "Will you be working here tomorrow?"

He stood, the ardent lover fast disappearing and the dynamic businessman returning. "Count on it." He captured her chin and looked down with cool determination. "And count on something else. You will live with me as my wife. Maybe not tonight. But soon. Very soon."

She didn't realize she was holding her breath until after he left. She released it in a great gusty sigh. Her situation became trickier by the moment. How long could she hold him off? How long did she *want* to hold him off?

The phone rang again and she picked it up automatically. "Constantine's."

"Ms. Constantine? Jack Maxwell here."

"It's Mrs. Thorsen now," she corrected him. "I married Thor Thorsen a little over two weeks ago."

There was a long pause. "Of Thorsen's Produce Markets?" he asked.

"The same."

"I guess it doesn't pay to leave town." He chuckled. "Shall I assume you aren't interested in selling your wholesale business anytime soon?"

"'Fraid not," she concurred.

"I'm sorry to hear that." He seemed to regroup. "I've met your husband a time or two, did he mention? He's a good businessman. I'm sure he'll help put Constantine's back on track."

Her voice cooled. "Thanks for your concern."

"I worded that badly, didn't I?" he said. "My apologies. In time I don't doubt you'd have given your competitors a run for their money. This profession isn't particularly kind to a woman on her own. I'm glad you have someone already in the business who can help."

"Even if it means losing Constantine's yourself?"

"Even if it means losing Constantine's myself," the response came promptly. "I won't lie to you. I'd have been delighted to get your business at a bargain price. But I'd be almost as delighted to get it at a good price. If you ever change your mind, I'd appreciate first refusal."

The man shot straight from the hip. In each of her conversations with him, he'd been polite, blunt and honest. She liked that. "You're on. But I wouldn't count on it if I were you."

"A man can hope," he said, and hung up.

Andrea stared at the phone for several minutes, a smile playing about her lips. As she'd known, things always worked out in the end. A few weeks ago, her problems had threatened to overwhelm her, and Thor had suddenly appeared. If he hadn't helped, in all likelihood she'd have sold to Jack Maxwell. And loath as she was to admit it, she'd have been relieved to do so, despite her preference to run Constantine's herself.

She tapped the prisms dangling from her desk light, sending them spinning. Tiny lights flashed and danced off the faceted glass and her smile widened. Yes. Things always worked out in the end.

ANDREA DELIBERATELY worked late, knowing it would force her to stay at the warehouse. Her income for the month was nearly depleted, which meant she couldn't afford to spend another night at a motel. Besides, why should she?

No one except Willie knew about the loft. Hartsworth had been stopped. She could only come up with one reason for not returning. And it wasn't a very good one. She rubbed the bridge of her nose wearily. She didn't want to go back. She wanted to be with Thor.

She stood and stretched. *Come on*, she argued with herself. *Procrastinating won't do a bit of good.* One night in her old bed and—her lips twitched—all her fears would be laid to rest. Switching off the desk light, she locked her office and started for the steps to the loft.

"Ms. Constantine? I mean, Mrs. Thorsen?"

Andrea jumped, stifling a cry of alarm. "Willie, you scared me."

"I'm sorry. I didn't mean to, honest." He frowned in bewilderment. "What are you doing here? Did you forget something?"

"Not exactly."

He glanced around. "Is Mr. Thorsen with you?"

She hadn't anticipated this, and she should have. "Er, no." Inspiration struck. "I'm working late tonight and have to get an early start tomorrow. I thought I'd sleep in the loft instead of driving all the way home."

Willie looked dubious. "I don't think that's such a good idea, considering the break-in and everything."

"That was weeks ago," she said with more composure than assurance. "And Thor took care of it."

"Yes, ma'am, if you say so." The security guard cleared his throat. "Uh, Mr. Thorsen, he doesn't mind your being here like this?"

Her gaze slid away and she shifted uneasily. "Would I be staying if he did?"

"I suppose not." He tapped his thigh. "Gotta tell you, though. That doesn't sound like the Mr. Thorsen I know."

Time for a fast exit. "I'm very tired. I think I'll turn in." She smiled and edged up a step.

He stopped her. "You still have that crowbar I gave you?"

"I have it." She made it up two more steps.

"You keep it close, all right?" he continued doggedly.

"I promise."

He turned away, shaking his head. "Don't know about this," he muttered. "Seems mighty peculiar to me."

Filled with remorse, Andrea watched him leave. She hated telling fibs. It made her feel lower than low. Unfortunately she had no choice. She climbed to the loft and opened the door, flipping on the single light bulb. Looking around, she shivered. After Thor's house, this place seemed pretty pathetic. And even more lonely.

Determined not to give in to self-pity, she crossed to the hot plate, intent on having a cup of tea. She picked up the thermos and shook it. Empty. Not having the nerve to return downstairs and get more water, she collapsed on the bed. She didn't deserve tea. She didn't even deserve plain old water. It served her right to go to bed thirsty.

She stripped off her clothes and pulled on her red-and-white-striped nightshirt. Bravely crossing to the light switch, she flipped it off and then scampered for her bed, huddling under the covers. A second later she threw aside the bedding and hopped up. Running to the door, she groped along the wall.

Her hand closed around a heavy metal rod. Gotcha! Racing back to safety, she shoved the crowbar under her pillow and tunneled beneath the blankets. Now if anyone came for her, she'd be prepared.

For the next hour, suspecting the worst, she tensed at every little creak and groan the old warehouse made. Finally she settled down along with the building, her limbs beginning to relax. Sleep. She needed sleep. If she could just calm down long enough—

A loud bang directly below jerked her awake, and she scrambled upright, the crowbar clutched to her chest. Her heart started pounding.

It was only Willie, she told herself. He was worried. He was checking to make sure everything was safe. There was nothing to fear.

Footsteps sounded on the stairs. The measured tread hit the landing and continued up.

Six more steps to her door. She tried to swallow, but found her mouth had gone dry. If it was Willie, why didn't he call out?

Her eyes widened. Maybe it wasn't him.

Five more. Had she locked the door? She couldn't remember.

Four more. Her feet hit the cold wooden floorboards at a dead run.

Three more. She flew across the room to the door.

Two more. She tested the doorknob. It turned with ease.

One more. Desperately she fumbled for the lock.

The door banged open, throwing her backward, and an enormous dark shape filled the threshold. She screamed in terror, swinging wildly with the crowbar.

It never connected. A huge hand caught it mid-arc.

"What the *hell* do you think you're doing, you crazy woman?"

"Thor!" she gasped, and toppled over in a dead faint.

CHAPTER EIGHT

ANDREA AWOKE to find herself resting on the bed, surrounded by Thor, Willie and Marco. Two wore identical expressions of concern. The third was flat out furious.

"Are you all right?" demanded the furious one.

That he was also her husband she deemed most unfortunate. "I guess so." She frowned in resentment. "You frightened me."

"Consider yourself lucky if that's all I do to you. What the hell are you here for?"

She sat up, tugging her nightshirt into a more modest position. "To, er, sleep?"

"Just the night, she said," Willie muttered, shaking his head. "A little tiff, I figured. Wouldn't hurt to make a phone call to my cousin and mention where a certain husband could find a certain wife. If he had a mind to, that is."

"He had a mind to," Marco confirmed.

"And how."

"If you two would excuse us," Thor said, interrupting their running commentary. "My wife and I need some privacy. Lots of privacy. A whole warehouse worth of privacy."

Willie scrambled backward and made for the door. "Fireworks time. I'm gone."

"Ditto," said Marco, right on his heels. The door slammed behind them and their footsteps echoed a rapid, and fast fading, tattoo down the steps.

"Who speaks first?"

Not her. Forget it! "Not me. Forget it!"

A shark would have sold his mother to possess Thor's smile. "Good. Then I'll begin."

"Look," Andrea broke beneath the strain, "it's not as bad as it seems. I got tired of the motel, so I came back here. It isn't forever, only six months or so. I'll find someplace else after that. You don't have to worry. I'm perfectly safe. Willie's around to guard me and..." She gulped, her words drying up as completely as a raindrop in the Sahara.

He appeared... *very* angry.

"You've been living *here?* How long?" Thor fired the questions at her.

She squirmed. "Not long."

"How long?"

It took two seconds for her to cave in beneath his cold gimlet stare. "If I don't count the night at your parents' house and the Saturday and Sunday at your place and the two weeks at the motel—" she calculated rapidly on her fingers "—thirty-two days, eighteen hours and forty-six minutes. I don't know how many seconds. Honest, I don't."

"You've lost me. Though why that comes as any surprise, I don't know." He ran a hand through his hair. "Let's try this one. Why are you living here?"

"Because I sold Nick's house."

He leaned closer, his voice dropping. "Why?"

She grabbed her pillow, clutching it to her. Not that it offered much protection. Feathers didn't stand a chance against Thor's razor-sharp gaze. "I had to pay off a few debts. It was the only way to keep Constantine's afloat."

"Son of a..." He rubbed a hand across his jaw. "Let's start from the top."

"Let's not."

His eyes glittered a warning. "I'm not in the mood for games, sweetheart. So answer my questions. Nick left outstanding debts, correct? You didn't have the money to pay them off, so you sold your house. With no place to live, you moved in here."

Her chin jutted out to a dangerous angle. "If you know all that, why are you asking?"

He stood up and, dodging the hanging prisms, moved across the room as far from her as he could get. "What's the current status of those debts? Are they all paid off?"

"Not quite."

"How much, not quite?"

"There's one final loan with the bank. It's large." Her belligerent scowl dared him to ask how large. "And I won't be able to settle it for some time, but we can meet the monthly payments without too much trouble."

"You can meet the payments." He closed his eyes in disbelief. "But you can't afford a roof over your head. Is that it?"

"That's it." she admitted resentfully.

"I warned you what would happen if you took too much rope." He moved from his position in the corner of the room. "You've just hanged yourself, my love. Get up and get dressed. We're leaving."

"Now?"

"Right now."

Not daring to argue, she did as he instructed, yanking her clothes on over her nightshirt. "Okay, I'm dressed."

He folded his arms across his chest. "Bring along something to change into tomorrow. You'll need it."

She turned on him. "No, I won't. I can change here."

Only after the words had left her mouth did she realize how furious he still was. He started across the room, not stopping until he towered above her, his hands balled into fists at his sides. He glared down, his eyes wild with barely tempered rage. She didn't dare move.

"Within the hour this room will be stripped and padlocked," he bit out in a voice that sent shivers down her spine. "You will not step foot in it ever again, not as long as you're my wife."

"You can't," she protested. "This has nothing to do with you."

"I say it has!"

"You have no right to tell me where to live!" Hurt overcame discretion, the words flooding from her. "You aren't really my husband. We only married to save your precious Milano account. It's not like you care about me or anything."

"Don't care?" He grabbed her. For an instant she thought he'd shake her. Instead, he swept her into his arms, hugging her close. The fury seemed to drain from him. "Dear Lord," he whispered. "Are you totally without sense? Of course I care. Don't you realize what Hartsworth's men would have done if they'd found you here? Alone?"

"You fixed all that," she murmured, cradled within the security of his embrace and unwilling to budge. "You said they wouldn't bother me anymore."

"And they won't. Because you're moving in with me. Period. No compromises. No discussion. No more arguments. You'll stay right where I can keep an eye on you, where I'm sure I can protect you."

Protect her, not the business, he'd said. Hope stirred. Maybe he was concerned. A little. "All right." She gave in gracefully, trying not to sound too happy about it. "But I get my own bedroom."

"Fine. The room's all yours. We'll share the bed."

Her eyes widened. "Wait one little minute here—"

"There seemed to be some doubt in your mind about the genuineness of our marriage." He smiled tightly. "I thought I'd end those doubts once and for all."

She choked. "I don't doubt it anymore. Honest, I don't."

He ignored her. "What was it you said?" His brows drew together. "Something about my not being a real husband?"

"You must have misunderstood," she claimed, desperate. "The acoustics are terrible in here."

He continued without pause. "I thought I'd prove to you how real a husband I can be."

"That's not necessary."

"Believe me, it'll be my pleasure."

She yanked free of his arms. "The hell it will!"

"Not quite, sweetheart," he corrected in a husky voice. "With any luck, it'll be closer to heaven."

Ignoring any further protests, he took her by the hand and marched from the loft. Downstairs, she caught Willie and Marco peeking from behind a board of oranges. She rubbed her backside and sniffed, satisfied by the look of horror the men exchanged. Served them right, finking on her the way they did.

"Cut it out," Thor growled. "I won't have it noised around that I'm a wife-beater." He stopped in his tracks and kissed her, not satisfied until she clung to him. "There. That'll give them something else to think about."

"Unfair tactics."

"Whatever it takes."

He bundled her into his car, and they drove out of the city. Neither spoke. Twenty minutes later, they arrived. The sight of his house filled her with equal parts relief and delight. She had not wanted to return to the loft. If there hadn't been a vague sort of principle involved, she would have stayed here from the very first night. Compromise could be good. But in this case, giving in was better.

He opened the front door and ushered her through. "You know where to put your things. It's late and we both have work tomorrow, so I suggest we go to bed."

She stood in the hallway, motionless, reluctant to move any farther. Did he seriously expect her to sleep with him? She could handle having him at the same workplace. She could handle having him in the same house. But no way could she handle having him in the same bed. She had to draw the line someplace. If only he'd stop erasing it every time she figured out where.

He glanced at her, his gaze softening. "What's wrong?"

"I, ah..." She studied the parquet flooring. "I won't sleep with you."

His footsteps came closer. He tilted up her chin and stared down at her. "Yes, you will," he informed her calmly. Before she could say another word, he added, "Not tonight. And not tomorrow night. And I doubt we will the night after that. But one of these days you'll be my wife in fact, as well as in name."

"Says you," she muttered for lack of a more intelligent response.

"Says me. For now, go to bed. You look like you're about to fall over."

And that summed it up to a tee. Feeling totally at odds with him, herself, Willie, Marco and the rest of the world, she went to bed. But she wasn't happy about it.

THE NEXT FOUR WEEKS proved the most difficult of Andrea's life. Giving up control to another person came hard to her. She'd lived under Nick's thumb for enough years to be unable to find any advantage in replacing a father's domination with a husband's.

Not that Thor dominated precisely, she hastened to correct herself. He more analyzed and decided. Unfortunately, if his decisions ran contrary to her own, she lost out. She was tempted to complain about his taking over so thoroughly. And she would have, too, if she could find something reasonable to complain about.

But with business booming, it didn't pay to gripe. Besides, how could she argue when he was always right? Right, not eight times out of ten, or eleven times out of twelve, but every single time.

It wasn't fair. Her employees all adored him. She'd learned more about the business in the past four weeks than she'd learned in the past four years. The quality of the produce continued to be top-notch. And costs were at their lowest point ever. Everything was so perfect it made her want to hit something—or some*one*.

That wasn't even the most annoying part. Worse still, he hadn't kept his promise to make their marriage real.

She glared at an innocent box of green peppers, and to add injury to insult, gave it a good swift kick. She sighed in exasperation. Nothing like creating your own distress sales from perfectly good produce.

"Uh-oh. Looks like trouble in paradise," Rainer called from the loading dock.

Andrea glowered until she saw who he'd brought. "Jordan!" She grinned, delighted. "I can't believe the old ball-and-chain let you come."

The petite brunette crossed the dock, Rainer keeping his arm around her the entire way. "I didn't give him any peace until he agreed. He has business to discuss with Thor, so I hitched a ride."

Rainer paused by the steps. "She's allowed to walk to your office, sit, then return to the car. And she's to be accompanied at all times," he stated explicitly. "No exploring and no sneaking off."

As much as it went against the grain to acquiesce to any terms a Thorsen dictated, Andrea had to agree. "It isn't safe," she told her pregnant friend. "If something happened to you, I'd never forgive myself."

Jordan made a face. "I know. But I'm going crazy. I'm not even allowed to work at Cornucopia these days. My own produce market! Can you believe it?" She brightened. "Do you have any gooseberries? I have such a hankering for them. Maybe if we checked your specialty room real quick—"

Rainer blocked his wife's path. "You will walk to the office."

She chuckled. "I know. I know. I will sit. I will not explore. I will not sneak off. You're no fun anymore, Viking."

"Not when it comes to the safety of my wife and child."

Jordan glanced at Andrea, mischief dancing in her gray-blue eyes. "Notice he doesn't say 'son'? He doesn't dare for fear I'll spite him with twin daughters."

He put an arm around her ample waist and helped her up the stairs. "I'd love twin daughters," he argued cheerfully. "They'd keep you too busy to get in any more trouble."

Andrea watched them, envy bringing a wistful smile to her mouth. She walked over to Marco. "Make sure a flat of gooseberries finds its way into Rainer's car. My treat."

Marco beamed. "*My* pleasure."

By the time she went upstairs, the door to Nick's—no, Thor's—office was firmly shut. Trying not to feel left out, she joined Jordan. Her friend stood in the middle of the near-empty room, looking around in astonishment.

"Good grief," she said faintly. "You've been robbed."

"Bet you never knew what color my rug was, did you?"

"I didn't even know you had a rug. Or a desk." Jordan pointed. "Or that chair."

"Impressed?"

"I should say so. What happened to all the papers?"

Andrea grimaced, sitting behind the desk. "Thor. Who else? He decided I needed organizing. He sent me on an errand one day, and when I came back *this* is what he'd done to my office." She shook her head in disgust. "Can you believe it?"

"The animal!"

She wished. "I wish." She buried her face in her hands and prayed that her desk—her empty organized desk— would swallow her whole.

Jordan collapsed into a chair. "So, Rainer was right. There is trouble in paradise."

"Let's just say you're a long way from winning that board of grapefruit. All Thor ever thinks about is business." She shifted in her chair, restless and unhappy. "I know that's why we married, and it's important to get Constantine's whipped into shape. But sometimes it's not enough. I want more out of life."

"I understand completely."

Andrea winced. Jordan probably did, too. Business had been a major bone of contention in her relationship with Rainer. When the Thorsens had bought her market, it had nearly ended their involvement.

"Why does business always come first with the Thorsens?" Andrea demanded.

Jordan sighed. "With Thor, it's because of his father."

That gave Andrea pause. "His father?"

"Didn't you know? No, I guess not," Jordan said, answering her own question. "I don't imagine it's something Thor talks about much. It took me practically forever to drag it out of Rainer."

"What? What is it?"

"Thor blames himself for his father being in that wheelchair."

Andrea gazed at her friend, stunned. "Why? What happened?"

"An accident about sixteen years ago."

Thor would have been twenty, Andrea figured. "The accident, it was Thor's fault?"

"Not in my opinion. He'd come home from college for the summer to work at Thorsen's. His dad called. He needed help unloading a truck. Thor had a date he couldn't break and promised to help the next day. His father wouldn't wait. A pallet-load of apples fell on him."

Andrea closed her eyes, horrified. "That's how he ended up in a wheelchair?"

"Yes. Thor went crazy. He dropped out of college and took over the business. Rainer says things were really rough for a while. They kept Alaric in the hospital for over six months, and the business suffered while Thor learned the ropes. Eventually he turned things around and rebuilt it to what it is today."

"He never returned to college?"

Jordan shook her head. "No. And ever since, he's *always* put business first. Rainer thinks he's afraid not to. Of course, it's ridiculous. Nothing like that could happen again. Thor's been very careful to delegate responsibility and train future replacements for all the key positions."

Andrea couldn't believe it. It was almost identical to her own situation. Her father dying and leaving her to figure out the business couldn't be that much different from Thor's taking over before he'd been adequately trained. And they'd both struggled to prove their worth to fathers preoccupied with business. Why hadn't he told her?

Not that it explained his avoiding her for the past four weeks. He'd promised they'd... She froze. Surely she didn't want their marriage to be a real one? Surely she did. She loved the man. She wanted to share with him on all levels, not on a business one alone.

"I don't know what to do," she confessed. "I don't know how to get through to him."

"Just love him," Jordan suggested gently. "He's been the responsible one for so long. He's taken care of his family, of the business, of every problem that's come along. He needs a partner, not another dependent."

Another dependent. That was precisely what she was, and until she learned the ropes, she couldn't do a damn thing about it. "Thanks, Jordan. You're a good friend."

"Ain't I, though." Then on a lighter note, she added, "I'm usually the one who requires all the advice. It's funny having the tables reversed for a change."

"Not from where I'm sitting, it isn't," Andrea retorted with feeling. "Why don't we find our husbands?"

They went into Thor's office and discovered the two men poring over several sheets of paper. Both wore identical expressions of frustration.

"We've tried everything I can think of," Rainer muttered, "and he won't give an inch. Could we have missed something?"

"What's wrong?" Jordan glanced over her husband's shoulder at the papers they were studying. "Oh, trying to entice a new account." She wrinkled her nose. "Though why you'd deal with that Captain Alexander is beyond me."

"Alexander?" Andrea repeated. Where had she heard the name before?

"Tugboat account," Thor filled her in. "He operates a whole fleet of them, and the reason we're willing to deal with him is that he's worth twice the Milanos."

Andrea's eyes widened, suddenly remembering the old sour-faced man at her reception. How could she forget him? He'd spent most of his time pigging out on Joe's cannoli. "He's turned you down?"

"Flat," Rainer groused. "We've tried wooing him with everything in the book. We've stressed quality."

Thor's eyes narrowed. "And price."

"Fast service?" Jordan added her two cents' worth. "That's important to the tugs, isn't it? Don't they often have to leave on the spur of the moment?"

"Tried it," Thor and Rainer said in unison.

"So what's left?" Andrea asked.

Her husband sighed. "I can't believe I'm saying this but... giving up?"

"That's our cue to leave," Rainer announced, and patted his wife's stomach. "Our second Lamaze class is in an hour. Our instructor's going to teach us how to breathe. Thought I'd nailed the basics on that ages ago."

"Idiot," Jordan said with a laugh. "You're lucky she's letting you return after last week. You nearly caused a riot with those tomatoes."

"I thought juggling them would be a great distraction technique," Rainer said in a wounded voice.

"It would have," Jordan agreed dryly, "if you knew how to juggle."

Andrea watched them go, her gaze pensive. They made such a happy loving couple. She glanced at Thor. He continued to analyze the papers spread across his desk. Would she ever have anything similar in her life?

ANOTHER TEN DAYS PASSED and Andrea couldn't seem to break through Thor's wall of reserve. He worked from dawn till dusk and then some. She knew why, and could see no way of preventing what had to follow.

Soon Thor would feel confident enough in her abilities to switch the daily running of Constantine's over to her. Once that happened, there'd be no further call for him to work in Nick's office, so he'd return to Thorsen's. After another few months, he'd regain confidence in her financial stability. Slowly, but surely, he'd distance himself until . . .

Until he ended their marriage. Tears flooded her eyes.

"Mrs. Thorsen?" Marco stuck his head in the door. "Lumpers are unloading that shipment of lettuce. We've got slime. Will you come and look?"

"I'll be right there." She turned away and discreetly wiped her cheeks. Business first, she reminded herself. She mustn't give Thor undue cause to stick around. Tears welled up again, nearly blinding her as she hurried down to the loading bay.

She stood at the rear of the forty-foot tractor-trailer, watching as a dock worker, or "lumper," pulled off the first stack with a hydraulic pallet-jack. She'd placed this order, and she'd be very upset if someone pulled a fast one on her. With luck it wouldn't be slime at all, only a little mud from the recent rains. She stood on tiptoe, trying to catch a glimpse inside one of the cartons.

"Andrea! Look out!"

She moved. Fast. Thor moved faster. He slammed into her, knocking her to one side just as the top layer of boxes tipped and crashed to the cement floor.

"Thor!" she shrieked. She rolled over, expecting to see him crushed beneath a load of lettuce. Instead she found him on his knees beside her. "Are you all right? Are you hurt?"

"Yes. No. Are you . . . ?"

She burst into tears. "Which is it?"

Through blurred eyes, she saw the blood staining his jeans and the arm of his shirt. She raised a shaking hand to her mouth. *Oh, Lord, don't let me get sick. Not here in front of all my employees. Not when Thor needs me.* She wouldn't be dependent and clingy. She wouldn't.

"Where were you hit?" Thor asked, his hands sweeping over her.

She fought for equilibrium. "Nowhere. I'm fine, but you're not." She gave up the battle, wailing. "Oh, Thor, you're bleeding."

"Skinned knees and shoulder. Nothing serious." He stood and helped her to her feet.

Only then did she notice the silent horrified crowd surrounding them. "It's all right," she called. "No real damage done."

"Mr. Thorsen, Mrs. Thorsen, I'm so sorry," the lumper said, wringing his hands. "I didn't realize the stack was—"

"Forget it." Thor cut in. "It's not your fault." He turned to Andrea's head salesman. "Marco, take over, will you? We're going home for the rest of the day."

"You got it."

Thor practically carried Andrea off the dock. "You'll make the bleeding worse," she tried to protest, seeing the dark stain growing at his shoulder. "I can walk."

"Tough. I'm not letting you go."

The taut white line about his mouth kept her from saying more. She understood how he felt. She needed the reassurance of his touch, too. He settled her into the car before climbing in himself. It wasn't until they were driving home that she began to feel the bruises and aches emanating from every muscle in her body.

He parked in the driveway and they sat motionless. She sighed. "You can't get out, either?"

A wry smile touched his mouth. "Nope."

She pushed open the door and cautiously lifted one leg at a time. Several contortions later, she exited the car. "You'd think we were ninety, the way we're creeping along."

Thor groaned, inching out of the bucket seat. "Huh. Aunt Gerda's ninety and she can still do handsprings."

"Good for Aunt Gerda." She massaged her aching hip. "I couldn't do handsprings at sixteen. I'd be hard-pressed to manage even a somersault right now."

"A hot bath for you, sweetheart."

"Sounds great."

In her room, she eased off her shirt and jeans and peered in the dresser mirror. She'd bruised her shoulder and hip when Thor threw her to the concrete. A huge purple blemish showed above the edge of her bikini underpants. Carefully she slid her bra strap to one side and winced.

"Ah, sweetheart," Thor murmured from the doorway. "That looks painful."

She glanced up, startled. He stood there, a tube of salve in his hand, staring at the ugly abrasion on her shoulder. The tautness returned to his mouth.

"It would have been worse if the lettuce boxes had hit me," she said, trying not to feel too self-conscious.

"I'm not so sure."

"I am." She cleared her throat. "Your shoulder. Is it okay?"

"Just a scratch." He seemed frozen in the doorway, and she held out her hand, gesturing awkwardly toward the tube. "Is that for me?"

"Yes." He stepped into the room. "I'll do it for you," he offered.

Her hand dropped to her side and she stood motionless before him. "Thanks."

He squeezed some of the ointment onto his fingers and her eyes fell shut. Gently he rubbed the cool balm into the scrape. "Where else do you hurt? Here?" He lowered his head, his lips touching the joining of her neck and shoulder, just above the bruise. His hands spread across her back, tenderly probing, seeking each sensitive area.

"My hip," she gasped, shivering in his arms. "And near my knee." Carefully he anointed her bruises, one after another. By the time he'd finished her aches were long forgotten, desire a welcome substitute.

"Sweetheart," he whispered. "Don't make me wait any longer. When I think what could have happened today..." His arms tightened around her. "You could have been killed."

Her eyes darkened. "Or you."

"Then be my wife."

There was no decision involved and only one possible answer. She loved him. She wanted to give her marriage a chance, to commit herself to him in every way. She didn't care about the past. It was the future that counted. And she'd fight for a future with Thor.

"Yes, please," she said, as politely as though she'd been asked to tea.

There was nothing in the least polite about his response. He scooped her up into his arms and carried her to the bed. He lay down beside her and, with infinite patience and loving tenderness, showed her the true meaning of marital bliss.

"WHY DIDN'T WE do this sooner?" Andrea asked, curling up beside her husband.

"You didn't want to."

"I didn't?" She thought for a moment. "Why didn't you tell me what I'd be missing?"

He chuckled. "It loses something in the translation."

"Perhaps if you'd explained better, I would have understood."

"I can explain it again if you think it would help."

"Yes, please."

"...THINK he'd have preferred a son. Maybe if I'd been one, he'd have given me a better grounding in the business."

"I doubt it. My father didn't." Thor rolled over and rested on an elbow. "After his injury, I really had to hustle. We almost lost it all."

"You should have told me."

He shrugged. "What's to tell? I had a duty to my father and to my family. You don't discuss taking responsibility. You just do it."

Her brows drew together. "And is that what I am? A responsibility?"

He reached out and smoothed a tumble of wheat-colored curls from her face. "You're the best kind of responsibility," he said with a smile. "You're a wife."

"I don't want to be another duty or obligation," she whispered. "I want more than that from a marriage."

He was silent a long time. "Sometimes you have to take whatever's available and make the best of it." He turned to her. "Why don't we make the best of it now?"

"...TOOK ME about four hundred hours to build the one in the living room."

"Four hundred?"

"At a guess. There's a lot of little pieces."

"You carved them all?"

"Every last strake."

"So, this... what is it exactly?"

"It's a longship."

"A longship. You make it to scale?"

"Yup. I have a friend who's a shipbuilder. He showed me how and offered some assembly tips."

She tried to imagine the amount of time and effort, not to mention sheer determination, such an undertaking would require. "Why do it?"

His brow creased in thought. "I guess because it represents my Norwegian heritage, a heritage I take very seriously. The Vikings were an incredible bunch of people, and I'm related to them. Look at all they did. It reminds me of what I can accomplish with the right kind of drive and ambition."

"*You're* an incredible person yourself, Mr. Thorsen." She glanced at him shyly. "I'm glad I married you."

His eyes blazed. "So am I."

" . . . TOLD YOU about my ships. Explain all those prisms."

"That's easy. They're rainbow makers."

"Yeah? How so?"

"You know. Hope for tomorrow. Hope everything will work out in the future."

"Faith?"

She nodded. "Faith. Trust. But mostly hope."

"I like that."

"Me, too." She touched his gold hammer earring. "Strength and power?" she guessed.

He shook his head. "Determination."

"You keep hammering away until you win?"

"Not win. Succeed. There's a difference."

She looked at him quizzically. "There is?"

"Yes. When you win, someone else loses. When you succeed, you overcome obstacles and obtain an important goal. It's a subtle difference, I'll admit. But an important one."

"Hope and determination," she murmured.

He gathered her in his arms. "Together they're an unbeatable combination, wouldn't you say?"

"The perfect combination," she agreed.

"...YOU NEVER MENTIONED. What did Joe Milano say that changed your mind about our marriage?"

She sighed. "That you'd approached his father about breaking their contract with Constantine's. That you wanted them to deal directly with you, instead. And since Caesar wouldn't agree, our engagement was a shrewd business move. It would prove quite an advantage in the negotiations."

"Milano said that?"

"Don't blow up at *me* about it. You're the one who made the deal in the first place—"

"I did not," he interrupted in a clear precise voice.

"—and no, Joe didn't use those exact words. He said, and I quote, 'This makes very good sense. Yes. Very practical and good business. I like it. My father, he likes it. My brothers, well, they don't like it, but I—'"

"'Smack them upside the head for being stupid.'"

She giggled. Then her laughter died. She rolled onto her back and stared up at the ceiling. "I wasn't going to be used as a commodity. I wanted to marry for love, not business." Her tone turned sardonic. "You see how long that lasted."

Thor gathered her in his arms again. "I didn't plan on telling you this, but I think it's important you know."

She traced his chest with her hand. "What?"

"Nick offered you as a bribe to ensure the Milano deal— that's how much he wanted our business. He said he could guarantee your cooperation. I don't know why he made the offer, but I think he knew I cared for you and thought making you part of the transaction would keep me off balance during the negotiations." He cupped her chin, his gaze steady. "Milano wasn't referring to our engagement as a shrewd business move on my part. He meant it was a shrewd business move on your father's.''

For the first time, she believed him. For some reason, Nick had felt compelled to use her as a bargaining chip. She'd probably never know why. She slanted a quick glance at Thor, wondering if her hurt was mirrored in her eyes. "What did you say to his offer?"

"Not a single word. I kept my mouth shut and hoped like hell it would all work out in the end." He sighed. "Maybe I should have backed away from the deal—not done business with Constantine's. I don't know anymore."

"Then why did you ask me to marry you, if not for business reasons?"

He leveled her with an intense blue gaze. "Because I wanted to marry you."

Andrea hardly dared breathe. "Why?" she asked again.

CHAPTER NINE

"Because—"

The phone ringing beside them shattered the moment. With a muffled oath Thor rolled over and grabbed it. "Yeah, what? Damn. No, no. I'll be right there." He hung up and tossed aside the bed covers. "There's a problem at one of the stores. I've got to go."

"You're not leaving?" Andrea said in disbelief, sitting up and clutching the sheet close.

He spared her a brief glance. "There's an emergency at work. I'm needed."

"But . . . but *I* need you. We haven't finished our conversation." *We've barely started our conversation,* she added silently, *at least the important part.*

"I know, sweetheart. We'll finish it later." He pulled on his shirt and jeans with quick economical movements. Returning to the bed, he sat down, dropping a warm kiss on her mouth. "We have plenty of time. This has to come first."

She couldn't believe what she was hearing. "First, before us?"

"No. First, because that's where the current priority is." He smoothed her hair from her face. "There's a problem only I can handle, which means I have to be there. It shouldn't take long."

"Wait a minute. You can't just walk out like this!"

A frown furrowed his brow. "You wouldn't argue if it was Marco who'd called."

She started to kick back the sheet. "The emergency's at Constantine's?"

"No. But that's not the point. Next time it might be. You knew when we married there'd be occasions like this. No business runs itself. And now we have two of them to worry about."

She froze, staring at him in alarm.

How many times in her life had she heard her father use that line? *No business runs itself.* He'd always said it right before missing something in her life: the school play, her birthday, graduation and a multitude of other events, both large and small.

"Andrea..."

Tears gathered in her eyes. Tonight had been another important event. How could Thor get up and walk away as though it was nothing? She licked her lips, trying one last time. "Thor, please..."

He seemed torn, but resolutely shook his head. "I can't, sweetheart. You know why I won't let them down."

Yes, she knew. His father's accident. He couldn't live with himself if something similar happened again. She truly sympathized. But it didn't change how she felt.

"I understand." She forced out the words.

He kissed her again, his mouth lingering. "Thanks. I'll try not to be long."

She fell against the pillows, watching him leave. Wasn't this a fine pickle she'd gotten herself into? *A* pickle. A whole mess of pickles. A whole flock or swarm or herd of pickles. And they'd all landed square in her lap.

She'd done precisely what she'd sworn not to. She'd fallen in love and, to make matters worse, married a man just like her father. A man who put business before her.

She was almost as bad. He had only to mention Constantine's and she'd been ready to bolt from the bed. She buried her head in her arms. Even on their wedding day, they'd put business first. And tonight, on their true wedding night, business once more came between them. Well, why not? She'd married him for that very reason, hadn't she?

But it made her slightly ill knowing that not only was her husband like Nick, she was fast becoming like him, too.

THOR DIDN'T COME HOME that night.

The next morning, Andrea got up and dressed for work. She glanced in the mirror and groaned. Exhaustion and a multitude of bruises from her rude encounter with the concrete dock had left their mark. Tempted to crawl back into bed and sleep for a week, she forced herself to walk from the house, instead. Worse, she forced herself to do it coffee-less.

Only then did she realize she'd left her car at Constantine's. Screaming won't do any good, she told herself. She cut loose with a bellow of frustration, anyway. Let the neighbors think what they liked.

She stomped into the house, snatched up the phone and began to dial. "I'm calling a cab, and I'll never, ever drive home without my car again." She paused, glaring at a philodendron. That didn't sound right. "Be *driven* home without my car. *Be* without my car. Dammit, I know what I mean!"

"I'm glad you do, lady, 'cause I haven't a clue. You after a cab or what?"

"You're a cab company, aren't you?" she snarled. "Why else would I call, if not for a cab?" The dial tone assaulted her ear and she hit the plunger half a dozen times. "Hello? Hello?"

"Hello, yourself," Thor said, dragging in through the open front door.

She slammed down the receiver. "Do you know what time it is?"

"Half-past six."

"I don't mean *that* time. I mean, do you realize how late it is?"

He blinked. "I thought six-thirty was early."

"Well, it's not! It's late. Where were you? What took so long?"

"At work, working."

"That's it? That's all I get? We make love for the first time in our life and you leave, only to slither back in with that pitiful excuse?"

"Forgot the coffee again, huh?"

She ground her teeth. "And what if I did?"

"Maybe you should write it down or something, so you'll remember next time."

Good. A fight. She'd worked up a full head of steam and was raring to cut loose. How kind of Thor to offer her the perfect opening. "Let me tell you what I'll remember to do next time—"

He grinned sleepily. "Sounds great. Don't worry about work. Everything's fine. I'm going to bed." He tossed her his keys and yawned. "Take my car. I'll call a cab when I wake up. 'Night."

"You—I—we—"

She watched, openmouthed, as he stumbled in the direction of his room, fell facedown onto the bed and began to snore. She debated for two solid minutes about whether to leave him there as he was. No. She couldn't let herself do it. Shoes had to come off at the very least.

By the time she'd finished, more than that had been removed. Thor lay in the middle of the bed, a coverlet wrapped around him and a blissful smile on his face. She stormed from the room, furious with herself for wilting over that smile. She'd turned into a total pushover.

She took his car without a single qualm and found things at work humming along. Thor's changes had wrought miracles, she acknowledged, checking the coolers before going to her office. Okay, so he put business first and she'd prefer it otherwise. He had reason. A lot of people depended on him. She sat down and gave her prisms a little spin. That didn't mean, given time, they wouldn't resolve their problems. She still had hope.

Or so she thought until she opened the notice from the bank.

She stared at it in disbelief. This couldn't be right. Ten days to pay off the loan? What were they talking about, ten days? Loans didn't work like that. There must be some mistake.

She called the loan officer listed on the request, drumming her fingers nervously against the clean, shiny—empty—surface of her desk.

"Mrs. Callum. May I help you?"

"This is Andrea Constantine—Thorsen," she corrected quickly, relieved that Thor hadn't been around to hear her slip. "From Constantine's Produce. I received a notice in the mail requesting payment in full of our loan. I think there's been an error. You see I've—"

"One minute, please."

The wait drove her crazy. Didn't the bank know what requests it sent out? How many loans this size did they have? Darn it, this information should be right at her finger—

"Miss Constantine?"

"Thorsen. *Mrs*. Thorsen."

"Quite. I'm afraid there's no mistake, *Mrs.* Thorsen. We did send you a notice, and you do owe us the, ah, figure mentioned."

Discreet. Very discreet. The witch. "But this is an ongoing loan," she protested. "How can you just call it due? I've been making my payments."

Mrs. Callum gave a light laugh. "Of course you have. Otherwise we'd have foreclosed on your business long ago. The point you're missing is that you don't have a loan."

"What do you mean I don't have a loan?"

"Temper, temper, Mrs. Thorsen. Getting angry won't solve a thing."

Except give her an immense amount of satisfaction. The loan officer remained ominously silent, and Andrea gritted her teeth, knowing what the rotten woman expected. Pride truly was a horrible demon. "I'm sorry." She pushed the words out with more effort than it took to move a mountain of spuds. "You were saying?"

"Yes, well," came the smug acceptance, "what you have is a line of credit. There's a difference, you know."

Andrea shut her eyes. "No, I didn't know. Why don't you explain the difference to me?"

"Certainly. A loan is a set amount of money we lend you at an agreed-upon interest rate for an agreed-upon length of time," she defined officiously.

I'm not an imbecile! Andrea almost shrieked. "I'm not an im—" she clenched her hands into fists "—er, following you. Isn't that what my father did?"

"No."

"No?"

"No. He set up a line of credit. That's money available for his use any time he needs it, up to a certain amount. If he dips into that money, he must make monthly payments as you've done. Once a year, the balance comes due and we decide at that time whether to extend the line of credit for another year." There was a long significant pause. Then she added, "As you've noticed, we've decided. And we're not."

Not? Andrea waved her fist at the phone. She'd give the old bat a knot—like the knot around a hangman's noose. Let her choke on that one awhile. "Why won't you extend our credit?" she asked, instead, impressed by her own forbearance.

"The quarterly reports you've sent us, your profit-and-loss statements and balance sheets, all show steady losses since your father's unfortunate demise. Frankly, Mrs. Thorsen, you're a bad risk."

She was *not* a bad risk. She *used* to be a bad risk. But ever since Thor fixed things at Constantine's, she was an excellent— Her eyes widened. Of course! Thor Thorsen, the man with the magical name.

"Perhaps there's something you haven't taken into consideration," Andrea suggested smoothly.

"I can't think what that might be."

"My marriage. I'm married to Thor Thorsen of Thorsen's Produce. You *have* heard of their markets?"

The change was instantaneous. "Mrs. *Thorsen.* I should have put two and two together."

"Why should you have put two and two together?" Andrea said pleasantly. *You only deal with numbers on a daily basis.* "You only—*we* only married a short time ago."

"In that case, we'd be delighted to review your line of credit," Mrs. Callum declared, charm itself. "Have your husband come down and we'll discuss the matter with him."

"You mean with *us,*" Andrea said. She didn't like being relegated to the background. Not when she owned the business concerned.

"That's not necessary. I'm certain your husband and I can work something out, especially if he decides to transfer his accounts to our institution. Shall we say Monday at nine?''

Andrea hesitated, unable to understand her reluctance to confirm the appointment. It was perfect. She only had to agree, and Constantine's would once more be on track. Salvation stood one word away. All she had to say was...

"No." That was one word, true. It just wasn't the right word. Her eyes narrowed. Or perhaps it was.

"I—I'm sorry?" Mrs. Callum stuttered.

Andrea sighed. "Yeah, me, too. Thanks, anyway, but I'd like to speak to my husband first. I'll call and let you know about that appointment,'' she said, and hung up on the woman's angry protests.

She stood and crossed to the windows overlooking the warehouse floor. As forklifts shifted boards of Granny Smith apples from the docks to the cooler, she frowned pensively. Why didn't she say yes when she had the chance? It didn't make a bit of sense. If she was smart, she'd phone the Callum woman and confirm the appointment. What had stopped her?

She grimaced. A picture of Thor leaving their bed to answer an emergency at work had stopped her. So had the other images. Images of her father putting work before everything else in his life, of herself competing for his time against the demands of a business. They'd popped into her head before she could say yes to the loan officer, and she hadn't been able to block them out since.

Annoyed by her own indecisiveness, she left the office and went downstairs. A new shipment of tomatoes sat on the warehouse floor. She popped the slats off the crate and examined the produce. Full, red and unblemished, they made her mouth water just looking at them.

"Sweet mommas, aren't they?" Marco said, coming to stand beside her. "Your husband picked 'em up for a terrific price."

She stiffened. "Thor ordered them?"

"Yup. You sure can count on that man to come through in a pinch. Check the strawberries in cooler one. They'll bring tears to your eyes."

"Those are thanks to him, too?"

Marco stirred uneasily. "That a problem, Mrs. Thorsen?"

"No, no," she murmured. "I didn't realize quite how much we depend on his help." She fixed her head salesman with a keen stare. "Aren't you and Terry doing most of the buying now? I thought he'd trained you to take over."

The older man gave an abashed shrug. "He gets the better deals. And I'm not a man to argue with success."

"No. Why should you, since Thor's ready, willing and able to do it for us?"

She looked away, her jaw firming into a stubborn line. Now she understood what bothered her about the situation at the bank. Once more, Thor would have to bail them out. What had Jordan said? *He's been the responsible one for so long.... He needs a partner, not another dependent.*

Not another dependent. If Thor used his company as backing or collateral or whatever other guarantee the bank required, he'd be tied to her and Constantine's for years. That might make her happy as a pig in slop, but it wouldn't be fair to him. Because, she didn't doubt for a minute, Thor would feel obligated to remain her husband as long as it took to satisfy the bank. She'd wanted to save Constantine's for her father's sake, but not at such a cost. It wasn't ethical, it wasn't reasonable, and it certainly wasn't the proper basis for marriage.

Wounded pride? she wondered as she walked into cooler one. Was her personal demon preventing her from asking for the help she required?

She thought about it, thought long and hard. Finally she shook her head. She'd never tried to lie to herself about her various mistakes. And there'd been many. She could blame innumerous foolish decisions or impulsive actions on her pride. But not this time. This time her reasons were sound, if unpleasant.

She wouldn't have the Thorsens responsible for the huge sums of money she owed the bank. She wouldn't have Thor tied to her because of that money. She wouldn't compete with the business for his attention as she had for her father's. And she wouldn't have her future determined by that business, or more specifically by Constantine's well-being.

She'd done her best. She'd sacrificed a lot. But it wouldn't be her sacrifice alone if she continued to use Thor's assistance. He'd helped enough, not that he'd agree with that. But she knew it to be fact.

First he'd resolved her supply problem. Then he'd trained her to run her own business. Now he faced a financial crisis that wasn't his doing. What awaited him next? What new problem would rear its ugly head? She couldn't, and wouldn't, keep running to Thor for help. She wouldn't be dependent on him any longer.

So, where did that leave her?

Exiting the cooler with determined strides, she returned to her office. It left her one place and one place only. Out of business. It also meant she'd have to call on a certain Jack Maxwell and see if he still wanted to purchase Constantine's. And heaven help her when Thor learned of it.

IT TOOK THREE DAYS to hammer out an agreement with Jack. Thanks to all of Thor's hard work, he made a much better offer than he would have previously. But on one condition, Jack remained firm. He wouldn't agree to keeping the Thorsen contract in force.

"It truly is worth more money than servicing Milano's Restaurants directly," she tried again, wondering if he heard the desperate edge in her voice. "I wish you'd reconsider your decision."

He sighed. "Let me level with you, Andrea—" He broke off abruptly, and several long nerve-racking seconds passed before he spoke again. "No, I'm sorry," he said, his voice brisk and reserved. "The restaurant account is too valuable. I'll have to insist on maintaining it, instead of dealing with the Thorsens."

What had he been about to say? An odd quality in his words and tone nagged at her. If only she wasn't so tired. If only she wasn't so worried about the ramifications of her decision. She'd missed something. Something important, but she was darned if she knew what. "I . . . I understand," she murmured.

"I could split the Milano account off and buy Constantine's without it," he offered reluctantly. "But I couldn't offer you as much." He suggested an alternative figure. A much lower alternative figure. A figure that wouldn't enable her to pay off her debts.

She closed her eyes. "The Milano account's all yours, Jack," she agreed, knowing the decision literally doomed her marriage. "You understand I can't guarantee the contract for longer than a year?"

"A year's plenty. I'll keep them happy from there," he stated with absolute confidence.

"Then that satisfies the final condition. I assume our lawyers can take over?"

"Right. Send the appropriate papers tomorrow. It's a little late this evening." He chuckled. "For some reason my attorney won't work past nine at night."

She laughed automatically. "First thing tomorrow will do."

"I know it's none of my business, but I'm curious. What changed your mind about selling?"

She didn't mind his asking. Nor did she mind answering. "I found that one business per marriage is plenty," she said evenly.

"Tough decision," he sympathized. "If it's any consolation, it's a smart person who can keep their priorities straight. Thor's a very lucky man."

Tell *him* that. "Thanks. But he may not agree with you. He doesn't know about our deal."

"Oh." The single word spoke volumes.

"I'd appreciate it if you'd give me twenty-four hours before announcing anything. After that, it won't matter."

"Sticky predicament," he understated the case. "Good luck."

"Thanks. I'll need it. Until tomorrow," she added, and terminated their conversation.

She reached over and clicked off the desk lamp. She'd done it. She'd actually done it. She'd sold out. Burying her face in her hands, she allowed the tears to come.

She mourned the loss of Constantine's, the business that had meant more to her father than his only child. She mourned the loss of her marriage. For without the Milano account, Thor wouldn't need nor want her anymore. And she felt the sharp bite of remorse for letting her husband down, after all his hard work.

But in her heart, she truly believed she'd done the right thing. She wouldn't be another dependent. She wouldn't have him feeling obligated to pay back so much money. And she wouldn't allow Constantine's to come first in their life together. If they still had a life together.

She'd been wrong all those weeks ago when Thor first proposed marriage as a solution. She never should have agreed to marry him for anything other than love. He'd wasted so much time, trying to set Constantine's to rights. And for what? So she could steal the Milano account from under his nose? He wasn't going to take that well. Not well at all.

She sat up and wiped her eyes. She'd allowed herself the indulgence of tears. Now to pay the price. She had another job to complete before she told Thor what she'd done. She couldn't give him the Milano account, but she could try to replace it with something of equal value. She could see that he didn't lose everything.

With that in mind, she picked up the phone.

AN HOUR LATER, she pushed back her chair. She'd accomplished as much as she could tonight. Which left one final task. In thirty days, Constantine's would no longer be hers. Thor needed to know that. Soon.

"Andrea?"

She jumped, a gasp escaping before she could prevent it. "You have a very nasty habit of sneaking up on me," she complained in a breathless voice.

Thor leaned against the doorjamb, studying her. "And you always seem to be doing something you shouldn't. Like now, perhaps?"

She froze, staring at him. "Why do you say that?"

He smiled. "Those big brown eyes, sweetheart. They're at it again." His smile grew. "You *are* up to something. What is it?"

Not now. Please not now. She wanted a little longer before she told him. "Is everyone gone?"

"All gone. There's just the two of us. Alone." His voice dropped suggestively. "Why? What did you have in mind?"

Distraction tactics. Pure distraction tactics. Anything to put off the moment of truth. "I have to check on the bananas we gassed today."

He tilted his head to one side and studied her, a question in his gaze. "I'm not sure what one has to do with the other, but okay. I'll tag along, if you don't object."

Andrea nodded. "I'd like that," she said, and led the way downstairs. She pulled open the heavy door to the room where they ripened the green bananas. A tropical warmth filled the small space, the slight odor of ethylene gas still lingering in the air. She peeked through the slit on the top box and nodded, satisfied.

Thor shot her a puzzled look. "Can we go home now?"

Not yet. A few minutes more. "Not yet. I'd like a few minutes more to check on the stack in the next room. They were gassed a couple of days ago for Jordan's market. She's sending someone to pick them up tomorrow."

He sighed. "I had to marry a conscientious woman."

The room she entered was narrow and used mostly for storage. The thick door closed automatically behind them, sealing, though not locking them, in the narrow space. In one corner was a pile of burlap potato bags covered with a huge mound of discarded plastic wrap. Next to it were Jordan's bananas.

She pulled the lid off the first box and smiled. "Perfect. She'll be pleased."

Thor put a hand on her waist. "How about pleasing me?" He nuzzled the nape of her neck. "I've missed you these past few days. If there isn't some emergency at work to keep you away, there's one at Thorsen's needing my attention."

She hesitated, suggesting tentatively, "Too bad we have two businesses to worry about. It certainly would be simpler with one."

"But not as interesting." He turned her around and pulled her more fully into his arms. "Nor as profitable. You're exhausted, I can tell. You've been overdoing."

She leaned her cheek on his chest and let the moment slip away. More than anything, she wanted to cry again. Instead, she laughed. "I've been overdoing? You're the dynamo running two places. How do you do it?"

"It's the blue tights and red cape. Works every time." His lips lingered on the pulse at her throat. She shivered and he whispered urgently, "Let's go home."

"Yes, take me home." She remembered Constantine's at the last minute. Pulling away, she gripped his arm. "Wait! I—I have to tell you something first...."

His smile was indulgent. "Tell me what?"

She couldn't do it. She couldn't say the words that would turn the warmth and gentle tenderness in those electric blue eyes to cold anger. She lowered her gaze. "I wanted to tell you thanks. For all you've done. The suppliers and the ordering and the organization." She shrugged. "All of it."

"You're welcome." His hand ruffled the golden curls tumbling across her brow. "Come on. Let's go."

One night, she decided in desperation. She'd give herself one last night before she told him what she'd done. It wasn't fair, and it wasn't honest. But she'd take the chance, anyway, and never once regret. "Yes, let's go."

Twenty minutes later they arrived home. Not home, she reminded herself fiercely as they went inside. Thor's home. She twisted her hands together. She didn't have a home anymore. And now that she'd sold Constantine's, she wouldn't even have the loft.

"Andrea? What is it?" He cupped her chin, staring down at her with concern. "You look so strange. Are you feeling all right?"

Mutely she shook her head, sliding her arms around his neck. She pressed her lips to the strong sweep of his jaw, nibbling, dropping teasing little kisses on the corner of his mouth. She felt the tension building within him. A tension answered by her own. With a groan, he swept her up in his arms and carried her through to the bedroom.

"I've decided something," he muttered against her flushed skin.

"What?" She clung to him, drawing in the scent of him, reveling in the feel of him, losing herself in the power of his touch.

He lowered her to the bed. "I like being married." His lips found hers. "I like it a lot."

Her fingers curled into her palms. "I like it, too," she choked out. She moved beneath him, afraid he'd say the wrong thing and destroy their final moments together. Words meant danger. Words brought loss. She didn't want words.

"Maybe—"

"Shh." She covered his mouth with hers. "Later. We'll talk later. Love me for now."

"Like you've never been before."

The darkness became a protective cloak, their embrace a brilliant warmth. She savored each instant in his arms, and tucked the memories away to be cherished and treasured when he was gone from her life.

He'd given her so much these past months. Tonight it was her turn to give. She'd give him one last special moment to remember. She'd give him all she had left.

She gave him her heart.

CHAPTER TEN

THE NEXT MORNING Andrea slipped out of bed and quietly dressed. She stood for a long moment, staring down at Thor. Her husband. The man she loved more than life itself. The man she was about to lose.

His face retained its toughness even in sleep. He looked strong and powerful, despite his relaxed posture and sprawled position. Thick tawny hair swept his brow, hair she'd caressed only hours before. A dark stubble clung to his jaw, and she remembered the abrasive feel of it scraping her breasts.

She closed her eyes and summoned all her determination. What lay ahead wouldn't be easy. But it would be done.

In the kitchen she brewed fresh coffee. He'd need it. Her lips trembled. *She'd* need it. There should be an hourglass somewhere, she thought with an edge of hysteria, where the sand slipped relentlessly through the narrow opening to mark the pitiful amount of time she had left of her marriage.

She heard Thor moving in the bedroom and poured his coffee. Placing it on the table, she retreated to the far corner of the kitchen and leaned against the counter.

"Morning," he greeted her with a warm intimate smile. Striding over, he enveloped her in a tight hug.

She held her breath, bracing herself for his kiss. *Traitor! Hypocrite! Deceiver!* She trembled. He felt it.

A single brow quirked upward. "You all right?"

"Sure." She cleared her throat and tried again. "I'm fine. The coffee's poured."

He glanced over his shoulder. "Okay." He took the hint and, with a tolerant smile, sat down. He leaned back in the chair, his long legs stretched in front of him. "So, what's up?"

"I have to talk to you."

"Okay." He took a quick gulp of coffee. "Talk."

"I've sold Constantine's."

His mug hit the table, the hot liquid sloshing over the rim and onto his hand. He didn't say a word. Certainly not the words she expected. He didn't ask her to repeat the bald statement. He didn't rant and rave. He didn't even ask that all important question: why?

Instead a cold smile touched his mouth, reflecting the wintry coolness of his gaze. "Brilliant move," he acknowledged. "One I didn't anticipate. Stupid of me, wasn't it?"

She shook her head. "No! You say that like I'd planned to sell from the beginning. You're wrong." She didn't know why she bothered with the denial. He didn't believe her. Not for one tiny second.

He grunted. "Yeah, right. Whatever you say."

"Something unexpected came up and I was forced to sell," she offered feebly. Pride kept her from telling him about the bank loan—line of credit, she amended. Pride, and the fact that he didn't care enough to ask.

"Who?" At her momentary confusion, he elaborated, "Who did you sell to?"

"Jack Maxwell."

Thor nodded. "I know him." He smiled cynically. "Should I even bother asking about the Milano account?"

"It goes with Constantine's." She wished she'd obtained the means to make it up to him, so she could offer something in its place. But with nothing definite, she was forced to remain silent. She couldn't give him what she didn't have.

"That's it, then." He took another gulp of coffee and stood. "I have work to do."

Don't you dare cry! she ordered herself sternly. *Don't you dare.* "Wait." She shrank from the look in his eyes. "We have one or two other matters to settle. Our marriage, for one."

He laughed then. She almost covered her ears at the sound, but didn't quite have the nerve. "What marriage? You've decided everything without consulting me. I'm sure you've decided how to handle that minor detail, as well."

"We married because of the business . . ." she began.

His lips twisted. "And we'll divorce because of it, too."

So, their marriage ended. No discussion. No explanations. No angry exchanges. She slipped her wedding band from her finger and stared at it for a long time, tears blurring her eyes. With loving care, she placed it gently on the kitchen table.

"I guess there's nothing more to be said," she whispered.

"Not another word," he concurred.

She tried to swallow and couldn't. "It'll only take me a minute to pack," she offered. "Then I'll go."

Her voice almost broke. She couldn't risk speaking again. Nor could she look at him. She was too much a coward to face the fury and disgust and condemnation in his eyes. It took every ounce of her strength to move away from the table and walk down the hallway to their room, correction, *his* room.

She packed. The entire time, Thor stayed in the kitchen. Once done, she didn't seek him out. There wasn't any point. She hesitated by the front door.

Explain it to him! Tell him why you did it. He'll understand. Tell him you love him. Maybe it will make a difference.

She turned the doorknob. He didn't want her love. He wanted her business. And that was the one thing she couldn't—wouldn't—offer. She squared her shoulders and walked through the door and out of his life.

HE WAITED UNTIL he heard the front door close behind her. Then, with all the strength his arm possessed, he heaved his coffee mug across the room. It crashed against the wall and shattered, a thousand and one pieces raining onto the floor to mingle with the black flood of coffee.

A muscle worked in his cheek. Five jerky steps carried him to the kitchen table. He picked up her ring. Slowly his fingers closed around it, crushing it in his closed fist. The edges cut deep into his skin, but he didn't flinch. This pain was nothing. Nothing at all.

Had she ever taken off his ring? he wondered. He opened his fingers and stared down at the shiny piece of gold. His thumb stroked the delicate braiding. Had she ever guessed at the symbolism behind the braid, why he'd chosen that over a bland exterior? Had she ever noticed the words he'd had inscribed inside the band? He ran his index finger over the graceful flowing script.

Først kjærlighet...

He slipped off his own ring and read the rest of the phrase.

...siden arbeid.

He'd been wrong to choose those words. His gaze grew bleak. Very wrong.

WITH NOWHERE ELSE TO GO, Andrea returned to Constantine's. Knowing the loft was padlocked, she ordered Marco to bring her some bolt cutters. She climbed the stairs above the offices, and her head salesman followed, resembling nothing more than a whipped puppy.

Seconds later, the lock dropped to the ground with a thud, and she pushed open the door, stepping inside. The room was stripped clean. Nothing remained, not even so much as a single prism. She closed her eyes. Her prisms. Gone, just like her hope for the future.

With her arrogance and her pride, she'd taken the best thing in her life and thrown it away. Oh, her reasons were sound enough, but they made for a very cold bedfellow. She'd gambled and lost it all; she'd lost her father's business, her husband and her future.

She'd always believed in tomorrow offering new beginnings and new chances. She'd always tried to look for the bright side in the gloomiest of disasters. Why should today be any different? She groaned. She knew why. Because Thor was no longer a part of her life. And without him, it would be a very dull gray life indeed.

"Anything else I can do for you, Mrs. Thorsen?"

She caught her breath, her eyes widening. Mrs. Thorsen, he'd said. Not Andrea. Not Ms. Constantine. But Mrs. Thorsen.

Her mouth firmed. She needed that reminder. Wasn't her goal to stand on her own, not be dependent on Thor? Hadn't she also wanted to take their relationship off a professional footing and put it squarely on a personal one? There'd been a reason for that. She'd wanted to eliminate Constantine's as a thorn in their side. And she'd hoped to work by her husband's side as his equal, not as another burden. She'd achieved her independence, a little more thoroughly than she liked, true. So what should she do with it? Fight for what she wanted or give up?

"Andrea?" Marco prompted in an undertone.

"Yes," she murmured. "There is something else you can do for me." She turned around and pinned him with a determined gaze. "I'd like you to uncover everything you can regarding a certain gentleman at my reception...."

"How YOU DO THIS to him, huh? How you leave and say nothing? You lose another marble?"

"Undoubtedly. Could we forget my marriage for a minute? I'm tired of talking about it."

"I," Joe Milano informed her arrogantly, "am not."

"You still haven't answered my question," she said, intent on regaining control of their conversation. "Can you prepare it for me on a regular basis?"

"No problem." He finished checking his garlic supply and moved on to the tomatoes. "I make the cannoli with my eyes closed."

Andrea grinned, vaguely surprised her mouth remembered the movement. "I'd feel better if you did it with them open."

"They are wide open for now." He glanced pointedly at her left hand. "What you do with your ring? I not see it for seven whole days."

She glared at him, jamming her hand in her pocket. "I lost it, not that it's any of your business. Drop the subject, or I'm going to drop something on you."

"Yes?" He looked intrigued. "Tell me how you do this, please."

"The cannoli," she tried again. "What sort of notice do you require to get it ready?"

He shrugged. "A couple of hours. Who is this for, anyway? Your husband, maybe? You forget to say."

She hadn't forgotten; she'd purposefully neglected to mention it. "Not Thor. Someone else. You met him at our reception," she said, deliberately vague.

His eyes narrowed. "I meet lots of people. Which is this one?"

"The big guy." She cleared her throat. "With the big appetite."

"What, you nuts or something?" he demanded, heaving carrot tops at the garbage pail. "That crazy man stole all my best pastry. Forget it. He is pig."

"Actually he's very nice. And he loves your cooking."

"Cooking?" he roared. A carrot hit her instead of the trash. "You call what I do cooking?"

"All right, cheffing," she roared back. "He loves your *cheffing.*"

"Okay, this is better."

"Then you'll do it?"

"No."

"Damn it, Joe. I need your help."

He eyed her sternly. "Your mouth, it is gonna get you in big trouble. And I not help you win another man when you got a good one already."

"I don't want him for myself," she admitted, desperate. "It's for Thor. I'm trying to woo a client for him."

"Ah, this I understand. A client for your husband."

She bowed her head. "If you don't do this for me, he won't be my husband for long." She peeked at Joe from beneath lowered lashes.

"You lie very bad, *cara,*" he muttered. "You not deserve Thorsen. He is a good man. I like him."

"I like him, too," she agreed contritely. "And you're right. I don't deserve him."

Joe heaved a martyred sigh. "I do this, and maybe it help you find your lost ring?" he asked.

"Yes." Lord, she hoped so!

"Okay. It is done." He glared at her, shaking a carrot beneath her nose. "But you get the ring back soon, *capito?*"

She grinned. "Boy, do I *capito.*"

"I'D SAY THE CAMPS are evenly divided. For the last ten days, Rainer's talked of nothing but killing you. Alaric and Sonja have taken your side. And Thor..." Jordan's eyes sparkled with mischief as she deliberately refrained from finishing her sentence.

"Did you invite me over to tease, or are you going to tell me what he said?"

"Thor hasn't said a word."

Andrea sighed, not surprised. She'd expected as much. "And you?"

Jordan shifted in her chair and grimaced. "Honestly, I could just scream! How could you sell the business like that, without even warning him?"

"I—"

"I thought you loved him."

"I do—"

"If you'd sold off Constantine's and turned over the Milano account to him, it would be one thing. But did you? No."

Andrea sighed. "No."

"So why?" her friend wailed. "Why did you do it?"

She wanted to explain to Jordan. She'd like just one person to understand what she'd done and the reasons behind it. "I owed the bank a lot of money. It came due," she said simply, giving the excuse in a cool emotionless voice. "The only way I could pay it off was to sell Constantine's. Without throwing in the Milano account, I couldn't sell the business for enough to cover the bank note."

Jordan stared at her in disbelief, a protective hand splayed across her belly. "Good heavens. Does Thor know?"

Andrea shook her head. "He didn't seem interested."

"And you didn't tell him. Andrea! The Thorsens would have helped. All you had to do was ask."

Andrea's lips formed a stubborn line. "I know."

The petite brunette sighed. "That darned pride of yours. I always knew it would get you into trouble. Would it really have been so difficult to accept his help?"

"Yes, it would have been." It all came pouring out. "Don't you understand? That's been the whole basis for our relationship, one business crisis after another, with Thor rescuing me from each one."

"What's wrong with that?"

"I don't want him to stay with me because of the business." She closed her eyes, her hands clasped tightly together. "I want him to stay with me because he loves me."

Jordan shot her a shrewd look. "You think it's all business with him, don't you? You think he married you because of Constantine's."

"I know he did."

"I don't believe it. I never have. I think he loves you. I think the trouble at Constantine's provided him with a convenient excuse."

How Andrea wished she could believe that. Unfortunately the truth was far different. "I know he married me because of the Milano account. I didn't like it, but I went into our marriage accepting that as a fact."

"And now?" Jordan asked, shifting awkwardly in her chair.

Emotion brought a husky note to Andrea's voice. "Now I realize I love him, and I won't have a marriage without love. If I'd asked Thor to help me with the financial problem at the bank, it would have meant a long-term commitment. I couldn't allow that. I won't stay married just for business reasons.''

Jordan threw up her hands. ''Pride. You're choking on pride.''

''Call it what you will. If Thor wants a permanent marriage it has to be because he loves me, not because he's forced into it. I won't use Constantine's to hold on to a husband. Nor will I allow a business to define my marriage.''

A secret smile played around Jordan's mouth. ''Have you ever said this to Thor? You might be surprised by his response.''

Andrea shoved the curls from her face. ''We did discuss it once. He said he wouldn't have married me if it wasn't for Constantine's. That's plain enough, I'd say.''

Jordan looked astounded. Then her brows drew together. ''Your ring,'' she said sharply, pressing a hand to her stomach. ''Where's your ring?''

''I left it with Thor.''

''Get it back,'' she urged. ''There's something you don't know—'' She broke off with a small gasp.

Andrea ran to her friend, dropping down beside her. ''Jordan? Is it the baby?''

She gave a weak grin. ''Did I happen to mention that I'm in labor?''

''No. You didn't.'' Andrea fought for calm. ''How long?''

''Most of the day. I thought there was plenty of time. Rainer had some business errands—'' She winced and gave a self-deprecating shrug.

''And you didn't want to bother him. Business. Always business first with this family,'' Andrea muttered. ''Come on. Let's get you to the hospital. Which one?''

''Northwest. Do you know the way?''

"I know it."

"Call Rainer. He can meet us—" Jordan gasped again, cradling her stomach. "Your ring. Get your ring."

Andrea put a supportive hand under her friend's arm and helped her stand. "Why is everyone so worried about my ring? Forget the damn ring. First things first."

Jordan pulled away. "Promise me you'll get it, or I won't go."

She'd always heard pregnant women were strange. She now had proof positive. "I promise." Seeing the stubborn gleam in Jordan's eyes, Andrea said with more conviction, "I promise. Can we go now?"

"Please. But hurry and get it, or I won't win my grapefruit."

"I'M SORRY. Rainer Thorsen isn't in right now. Thor Thorsen is available, or you could leave a message."

"Put me through to Thor."

"Whom may I say is calling?"

"Tell him it's a family emergency and get him on the line. Now!" A series of clicks sounded in her ear, and then she heard Thor's reassuring voice. "It's Andrea," she said quickly. "I'm at the hospital."

"Are you hurt? Which hospital? I'll be right there."

There was no mistaking his concern. She squeezed her eyes shut, feeling a resurgence of hope. "It's Jordan. She's gone into labor. Do you know where to find Rainer?"

"Yes. We'll be right over." He didn't hang up, and after a brief pause, he asked, "Will you still be there?"

She laughed self-consciously. "Jordan made me promise I'd stay. I doubt your brother will be happy about it, though."

"You let me worry about Rainer. Don't move from that spot, you understand?"

Her smile turned wobbly. "I like it when you talk nasty."

"Then you're going to love our next conversation, sweetheart."

He hung up and Andrea leaned her head against the wall by the phone. At least they were talking. But for how long?

THE INSTANT Thor hung up, the phone rang again. "What is it?" he barked into the receiver.

"Same to you, and do I have some interesting news. Wait'll you hear."

"Not now, Rainer."

"Just listen to this—"

"Andrea called. She's at the hospital with Jordan. Your wife's in labor."

"I'm on my way."

"One thing first." Thor's tone hardened. "You say a single unpleasant word to my wife, and your life won't be worth dust in a high wind."

Rainer chuckled. "No fear of that, big brother. No fear at all. See you soon. *I'm gonna be a father!*" he shouted, and hung up.

Thor cradled the receiver and leaned back in his chair. Slipping his hand into his pocket, he fingered Andrea's wedding band and smiled.

Soon, very soon, he'd help that little lady climb off her high horse, even if he had to drag her down personally.

WHERE WAS EVERYONE? Andrea wondered for the hundredth time. She squeezed Jordan's hand and glanced at the clock on the wall of the birthing center. "Thor will find him. I know he will."

"You've told me that every minute on the minute. I believe you already. I believe you. Now let me concentrate on my breathing."

"Jordan?" Rainer pushed into the room and grinned at them, his arms overflowing with flowers. He dropped them at the foot of the bed and enclosed his wife in a tender hug. "How's my Valkyrie?" he whispered his favorite endearment.

"Your warrior maiden is busy breathing, Viking. About time you showed up."

He glanced over his shoulder at Andrea. "Hang on a sec," he said, stopping her before she could leave the room. "I have something for you, too." He picked up a bouquet of white roses and handed it to her.

Andrea stared in confusion. "For me? I don't understand."

"You do that innocent look very well." He chuckled, then gave her a jubilant hug, swinging her around in a circle. "Let me say one word before you leave. Cannoli."

Her eyes widened. "You know. Does Thor?"

"Not yet. I thought you'd like the pleasure of telling him yourself." He escorted her to the door. "And now, if you'll excuse us, we're going to have a baby."

"*I'm* going to have a baby," Jordan snapped. "And when I'm through there'd better be some grapefruit to show for all my trouble, or there'll be hell to pay."

Andrea blinked away tears. "I...I can't make any promises. But I'll do my best. Good luck." She wandered out to the waiting room and sat in a chair and, as the sign above the room decreed, waited. And waited and waited. Or so it seemed.

Just as she'd begun to lose hope, Thor showed.

She jumped to her feet. Attack being the best defense—and safer, judging by his expression—she let him have it with both barrels. "You've taken long enough!"

"You mean I've taken *quite* enough. Now you start taking."

"Fine. I'll start with my ring." She held up her hand and wiggled her fingers. "Put 'er there."

"You mean this?" He reached in his pocket and pulled out her wedding band. "Forget it."

She tried a different approach. "I'd like my ring back."

He flicked it into the air and caught it. "Tough."

She gritted her teeth against the prideful voice whispering in her ear. "Please, Thor, may I have my ring?"

He returned it to his pocket and shook his head. "Not yet."

"You . . . you want me to beg?" she choked.

"That would be nice." He laughed at her expression. "But, no."

She glared at him. "You'd like an apology? What?"

His laughter died, his blue-eyed gaze turning fierce. "An explanation, as you damned well know. I'd like an explanation about Constantine's, and I'd like to know why you want the ring."

"The explanation might take a while," she said, stalling. Not that it helped.

"I've got all day and all night."

"Excuse me, you two—" Rainer appeared in the doorway and glanced from one to the other, a huge smile on his face.

"You've finally decided you want an explanation?" she demanded, ignoring Rainer. "You didn't before. You let me leave your house without making a single move to stop me."

"You might like to know—" Rainer tried again.

"What was I supposed to say? You took off your ring and left. Comebacks to that are a bit hard to find."

"It's a girl—"

"How about, 'Don't go'?"

"Seven pounds, nine ounces—"

"Would it have made a difference?"

"Hair as red as a beefsteak tomato—"

"Yes, it would have made a difference," Andrea snapped. "It would have made all the difference in the world."

"Valerie. We named her Valerie. Get it? Valkyrie, Valerie." Frowning, Rainer glanced from his brother to his sister-in-law. "Maybe I can help move things along. Thor, you say: 'Why did you sell Constantine's?'"

"Yeah, right. Why *did* you sell Constantine's?"

Rainer nudged Andrea. "And you say: 'Because...' And fill in the blanks."

"Because, and fill in the blanks." The nudge became a shove. "All right. All right." She glared at Thor. "I wouldn't have business coming between us anymore. If we were going to stay together, it had to be for personal reasons, not business."

Thor ran a hand through his hair. "You sold because you wanted proof I loved you?" he asked in exasperation.

She eyed him uncertainly. "Er, no?" She glanced at Rainer. "That was a 'no' question, wasn't it?"

"Sounded like it to me."

Thor gritted his teeth. "You want proof? Fine. I'll give you proof." He grabbed her by the hand and started out of the room. "Congratulations, Rainer. A girl, huh? Tell Jordan she'll have that grapefruit delivered to her market first thing in the morning."

"You knew about our bet?" Andrea squeaked.

"I knew." He turned a hard look her way. "Not another word until we're home. And then you'd better talk fast."

The minute they hit the house, the torrent began. "I owed the bank a lot of money," she said, inching into the living room. "The note came due. It was either sell or have the Thorsens back Constantine's line of credit."

"Which you chose not to do."

She sighed, nodding. "Which I chose not to do. Thor, it was more than two hundred thousand dollars."

He couldn't hide his shock. "Two hundred— How the hell did that happen?" His eyes narrowed, sudden understanding in his gaze. "Nick wasn't quite the businessman we all assumed, was he?"

"No," she admitted. "He took chances, lots of them. He'd buy on spec in order to best his competitors, get a deal they couldn't match. For a long time, he did very well. But the last few years, that changed."

Thor rubbed a hand across his jaw. "Which explains why he went after Thorsens' business so ruthlessly. I never could understand what made him desperate enough to throw you into the deal."

She thought about it. Things must have been very tough financially for Nick to have used her like that. But it made sense. It made a lot of sense. She crossed to Thor's side and put a hand on his arm. "Don't you understand? I couldn't ask you to help with the loan. It was too much. Jordan says it's pride. I say it's practical. Constantine's wasn't worth it. Nor, in my opinion, was the Milano account."

He didn't pull away from her. Instead he cupped the side of her face, his fingers sinking into her hair. "But you made the decision without consulting me. Why?"

She shivered beneath his touch, struggling for control. "Because I didn't think you'd agree. Because you'd handled every other crisis that came our way, and I felt it was time to take care of matters myself. Because..." She closed her eyes, finally admitting the truth. "Because I was tired of the business always coming first in your life. It's selfish, I know, but *I* wanted to come first for a change."

"You are first." She shook her head, and he said more insistently. "You *are*. You'll notice the *first* thing I did was hustle you to the nearest altar. And then I married you in front of as many witnesses as I could stuff into that church. I wanted to tie you to me so tight you'd never be free of our marriage."

"But what about Constantine's? You told me, if not for the business, you'd never have married me. Explain that."

"Hurt, did it?"

She nodded, tears spiking her lashes. "Yes, it hurt."

His thumb caressed her cheek. "I asked you to marry me a year ago. How did you respond?"

She froze. "I..."

"You ended up saying no, remember? If it weren't for the problems at Constantine's, the answer would still be no. I had to blackmail you into marrying me. So I did. I used every excuse I could come up with. I wanted you that much." She couldn't mistake his sincerity. "You still haven't told me why you want your ring back."

A tear traced a path down her cheek. "I want my ring because I love you."

He reached into his pocket and handed it to her. "Look at it."

Remembering Jordan's obsession with its return, she examined the band. Instantly she found the inscription inside. "I never noticed this before." She licked her lips and glanced up at him. *Først kjærlighet...* What does it mean?"

"First love." He tugged off his ring and handed it to her. "And mine gives you my answer. *...siden arbeid.* Then business."

Andrea shut her eyes, sobs racking her slender frame. He scooped her up in his arms. "I love you, my prideful wife. I always have and I always will."

She buried her head in his shoulder, clinging to him as he strode toward the bedroom. "Welcome home," he whispered against her ear. "Hope, remember? You told me about its importance the night we made love. I've lived on nothing *but* hope these past days. And faith. Faith that you'd come back to me. And trust. Trust, that you loved me as much as I loved you." He set her on her feet. "And determination. I was very determined to succeed where you were concerned, my love."

She opened her eyes and looked around the bedroom. "Oh, Thor!" she whispered. Everywhere were prisms, her prisms and then some—hanging above the bed and on all the fixtures and in each window. The entire room was brilliant with colors—every color in the rainbow. And attached to each prism was a tiny gold hammer. "Hope and determination," she whispered, remembering their first night together.

He crushed her in his arms. "An unbeatable combination. I love you. Not for Constantine's. Not because of the Milano contract. But for you."

She suddenly remembered. She hadn't told him about the tugboat account. She wrapped her arms around his neck. There'd be time. Plenty of time. Right now, business would have to wait. They had more important matters to take care of.

EPILOGUE

"THIS IS THE SWEETEST grapefruit I've ever tasted!" Jordan exclaimed.

Andrea grinned. Cradling Valerie in her arms, she gently ruffled the red-gold curls. "Believe me, it's my pleasure."

"Cannoli, anyone?" Thor asked, holding out a platter. "Joe dropped it off as a gift for the new momma and to say he's delighted the Thorsens are once again his suppliers."

"Here I busted my buns getting that tugboat account for you, bribing Captain Alexander with Joe's cannoli, and for what?" Andrea complained. "Jack Maxwell intended to hang on to the Thorsen contract all along. He's a sneaky man."

Thor took a huge bite of pastry. "No. He's an astute businessman. A very astute businessman. By refusing to make Thorsen's Produce part of the sale, he forced us to renegotiate our contract. Which put him in a stronger bargaining position."

She remembered again her final worrisome discussion with Constantine's new owner. She knew she'd missed something vital during that telephone conversation, and now she knew what. It must have been very difficult for Jack to keep quiet about his intentions, considering his innate honesty. "And did he get a better deal?"

"A bit. There's one other little difference with this arrangement." He grinned wickedly. "I didn't get a wife out of it."

"You didn't before," she scoffed. "I nixed that particular deal, if you'll recall."

"Well, there won't be any more of that nixing stuff. You promised."

She frowned. "When did I do that?"

"You don't remember? You mean to tell me you stood before a pastor with thousands of witnesses and don't even remember what you promised?"

"It was hundreds, not thousands. And I promised to love and honor," she retorted. "That's it."

"And be protected. And to live together. We discussed that part on our wedding night. And no nixing of deals."

"I never—"

"The minister said it in—"

"Norwegian, right?"

"You got it." He counted off on his fingers. "Love, honor, protect, live together, no nixing of deals and obey."

She handed the baby to Rainer and crossed to stand in front of Thor, her hands on her hips. "I *never* promised to obey. *Never.*"

Thor's mouth tightened in a stubborn line. "'Obey' was in there someplace. I remember it."

"Distinctly," Rainer threw in.

"In Norwegian," Thor added. "That's why you don't recall."

"Rainer always claims I promised to do the dishes," Jordan said with a laugh.

"That's a good one. I like it," Thor approved. "And do the dishes."

"That's it?" Andrea demanded. "Love, honor, protect, live together, no nixing deals, obey and dishes. That's everything?"

He stood and enfolded her in his arms. "That's everything."

Andrea grinned. "I'm relieved to hear it." Maybe she'd learn Norwegian. Yes, that was precisely what she'd do. Then she'd add one or two vows of her own.

He cupped her chin. "At least, that's everything until I remember something else. Like the two of us working together for the rest of our days. Because working with you, business would always be a pleasure...."

She chuckled. "With pleasure always coming first."

"You got it, love. You got it."

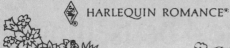

® HARLEQUIN ROMANCE®

**Harlequin Romance
knows you love
a Western Wedding!**

And you'll love
next month's title in

THE BRIDAL COLLECTION

SHOWDOWN! (#3242)
by Ruth Jean Dale

THE BRIDE was down-home country.
THE GROOM was big-city slick.
THE WEDDING was a match made in Texas!

Wherever Harlequin Books are sold.

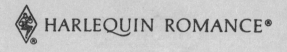

HARLEQUIN ROMANCE®

Norah Bloomfield's father is recovering from his heart attack, and her sisters are getting married. So Norah's feeling a bit unneeded these days, a bit left out....

Orchard Valley

And then a cantankerous "cowboy" called Rowdy Cassidy crashes into her life!

"The Orchard Valley trilogy features three delightful, spirited sisters and a trio of equally fascinating men. The stories are rich with the romance, warmth of heart and humor readers expect, and invariably receive, from Debbie Macomber."

—Linda Lael Miller

Don't miss the Orchard Valley trilogy by Debbie Macomber:

VALERIE   Harlequin Romance #3232 (November 1992)
STEPHANIE   Harlequin Romance #3239 (December 1992)
NORAH   Harlequin Romance #3244 (January 1993)

Look for the special cover flash on each book!

Available wherever Harlequin books are sold.   ORC-3

HARLEQUIN
HISTORICAL
CHRISTMAS
•STORIES•1992•

Capture the magic and romance of Christmas in the 1800s with HARLEQUIN HISTORICAL CHRISTMAS STORIES 1992, a collection of three stories by celebrated historical authors. The perfect Christmas gift!

Don't miss these heartwarming stories, available in November wherever Harlequin books are sold:

**MISS MONTRACHET REQUESTS by Maura Seger
CHRISTMAS BOUNTY by Erin Yorke
A PROMISE KEPT by Bronwyn Williams**

Plus, as an added bonus, you can receive a FREE keepsake Christmas ornament. Just collect four proofs of purchase from any November or December 1992 Harlequin or Silhouette series novels, or from any Harlequin or Silhouette Christmas collection, and receive a beautiful dated brass Christmas candle ornament.

Mail this certificate along with four (4) proof-of-purchase coupons plus $1.50 postage and handling (check or money order—do not send cash), payable to Harlequin Books, to: **In the U.S.:** P.O. Box 9057, Buffalo, NY 14269-9057; **In Canada:** P.O. Box 622, Fort Erie, Ontario, L2A 5X3.

**ONE PROOF OF
PURCHASE**

Name: _____

_____

Address: _____

_____

City: _____

State/Province: _____

Zip/Postal Code: _____

HX92POP   093 KAG